GAME

BLACKWINGS
DEVIL SPRINGS

TEAGAN BROOKS

GAME

BLACKWINGS MC - DEVIL SPRINGS - BOOK 8

TEAGAN BROOKS

Adult Content Warning: For ages 18 years old and older due to graphic sexual content, explicit language, and violence.

BLURB

Game

At the age of eighteen, I moved out of my mother's house and ended the toxic relationship I had with my family. Then, I joined the Blackwings MC and found the family I wished mine could have been. We're a brotherhood and always there for each other. When Judge needed help getting caught up on orders at his security company, I was happy to help. I had no idea that one of his customers would steal my heart with her worry-filled eyes and a glass of lemonade.

Blakely

When both of my parents abandoned me as a newborn, my grandparents stepped in and raised me. Years later, when my grandparents retired, they decided to travel the country and left me to run their storage unit facility. Everything was going great until my estranged half brother showed up unannounced and asked me if he could put his belongings in one of my units while he served thirty days in jail. Oh, and he also wanted to leave his three-month-old son with me. I shouldn't have agreed. But I did, and that's when the trouble started.

To my daughter and my bonus daughter

ACKNOWLEDGMENTS

Cover Designer: CT Cover Creations

Special thanks to M Merin, Brittany Franks, and Heather Whitaker.

PROLOGUE

GAME

I picked up my ringing phone and glanced at the name on the screen before immediately silencing it and dropping it onto the bed. I couldn't remember the last time I'd spoken to my mother, and I wanted to keep it that way. Unfortunately, she had other plans.

As soon as the phone stopped ringing, it started again. She called two more times before I finally answered.

"What?" I barked into the phone.

"Grant, I need your help," she said.

"Of course you do. Why else would you call?"

"Dani's missing."

"And?"

"What do you mean 'and'?" she huffed. "We have to find her."

"No, *we* do not have to find her. She's probably holed up with a guy somewhere. I'm sure she'll turn up soon."

It wasn't the first time my niece had gone *missing,* and I was sure it wouldn't be the last.

"This is different," she countered. "No one's seen or heard from her for over a month."

"Yeah," I said slowly. "I'm not seeing how this is any different."

"Some man came by here looking for her. He said she has something of his, and he needs it back. He didn't seem like a good person."

"I really don't know why this is so hard for you to understand, but I don't care. She made her bed, with your help, and she can lie in it."

"I just thought those bikers you hang around with might know something."

I laughed derisively. "I can assure you they don't. They don't associate with the kind of people Dani does."

"So, you're not going to help me?"

"I'm not sure how many different ways I need to say it, but no, I'm not. I stopped caring what happened to her a long time ago. Nothing you say or do is gonna change that."

"I didn't raise you to treat your family this way."

"No, you raised me to allow family to treat me this way. Which is why I chose a new family. Take care, *Mother,*" I said and disconnected the call.

I really didn't care what kind of trouble my niece had gotten into. At one time, I did, but that all went out the window shortly after she came to live with us when my older sister was arrested and sent to prison.

I was a surprise baby born eighteen years after my

sister and only a few years before my niece. Dani spent a lot of time with us when we were growing up, but she didn't live with us full time until I was fifteen. And that's when things started to change. She'd always been a difficult child to deal with, but it seemed to increase tenfold once she moved in, and I was the only one who could see it.

My mother thought she was the golden child who could do no wrong. When in reality, Dani was always doing wrong and manipulating the situation to make herself look innocent. She thrived on creating conflict between other people so she could sit back and watch. At first, I thought she did it for entertainment, but as I got older, I realized she did it for an entirely different reason. She wasn't a likable person, so she created situations to get everyone upset and keep the attention off of her. When the focus was elsewhere, she could do whatever she wanted without repercussions.

It worked for years, and it probably still did to some extent. However, I caught on to what she was doing and started pointing it out. At first, my mother made excuses for her behavior, but eventually, she ignored it and acted like I was the problem. I wasn't going to hang around while my mother refused to listen to reason and continued to propagate my niece's bullshit. When I'd finally had enough, I moved out and washed my hands of them. Then, I joined the Blackwings and found the family I wished mine could have been.

Blood might be thicker than water, but blood is much more toxic than water will ever be.

* * *

Two Days Later

"Hey, Game, there's two detectives at the front desk asking for you," Coal said from the side of the boxing ring.

I sighed and started removing my gear. "I'll be right there."

It didn't take long for me to reach them, but it was more than enough time for me to become well and truly irritated by the time I did. "Can I help you with something?" I asked, trying and failing to hide my annoyance.

"Are you Grant Summers?" one of the detectives asked.

"Yes," I confirmed.

"I'm Detective O'Brien, and this is my partner Detective Higgins. We're working on a missing persons case, and your name was given to us—"

I held up my hand. "Let me stop you right there and save us all some time. I haven't seen or spoken to Dani in three or four years. I have no idea where she could be. In short, I have nothing to do with any of my blood relatives, so I'm not sure why my mother gave you my name."

One of the detectives arched his eyebrow. "What makes you think your mother gave us your name?"

I snorted. "Because she called me two days ago asking me to help her find Dani, and I refused. Now, you're here asking questions."

"Is there anything you can tell us that might be helpful?"

"Dani's done stuff like this before when she didn't get her way. She'd disappear for a while. Then, she'd return, and my mother would be so relieved that she'd give her whatever she wanted. I cut ties with them a long time ago, but I highly doubt that cycle has changed," I explained.

"Well, if you think of anything else or happen to hear from her, please give us a call," the older detective said and handed me a business card.

"Will do," I said and waited until they left to toss his card in the trash.

"What was that about?" Bronze asked.

"My niece is 'missing,' and they were asking about her."

"You don't think she is?"

"No, and even if she was, I wouldn't know anything. I haven't spoken to her in years," I explained.

He nodded once. "Let me know if this becomes a problem."

"Thanks, but I don't think it will. They were just following protocol," I said and got back to work.

1

BLAKELY

"I'll wait until you get back," Landon said as I headed out the door.

"You don't need to," I told him for the umpteenth time. "I'll be fine."

"We've already had this conversation. Since you won't let me go with you, I'm staying and that's that. Go see what this guy wants. I need to know if I can go home and get ready for my date or if I should prepare to be on the news."

I shook my head at his dramatics and went out to meet a potential customer at an available unit. Landon felt the need to stay because this particular customer specifically requested to have the manager meet him at the unit instead of coming to the office. Even though it was an unusual request, I didn't think it was a problem, but something had made Landon's hackles rise.

Since the unit was near the back of the property, I took the golf cart we kept around for that very reason. I arrived before the customer so I could open the door and turn on the light. There wasn't much I could do to stage a storage unit, but based on my own research, a customer was more likely to sign a rental agreement if the light was on when they arrived.

"Hey," someone said from behind me.

I gasped and turned around, surprised to see my estranged half brother standing there holding a baby. "Ben?"

"Yeah, it's me," he cleared his throat and took a few steps closer. Then, he tilted his head toward the baby in his arms. "Um, this is my son, Kalen. And we need your help."

"My help?" I blurted. I couldn't imagine what kind of help he could possibly need from me. We didn't have a relationship. We were practically strangers.

"Yes," he nodded.

I waited for him to start explaining. When he didn't, I placed my hands on my hips impatiently. "Are you going to tell me what kind of help you need? Or how about why you came to me?"

He extended one hand and gestured for me to stop with my rapid-fire questions. He glanced over his shoulder as if he was making sure the coast was clear before he spoke. "I came to you because I need a storage unit," he said simply. Then, he stepped closer and lowered his voice. "The truth is, I got into some trouble, and I have to serve thirty days in jail. I can't keep my apartment while I'm in jail, so I need somewhere to put my stuff, and I need someone to watch him until I get out."

I couldn't hide the look of shock on my face upon

hearing his words. "What kind of trouble are you in?" I nearly whispered.

He waved his hand dismissively. "It's nothing major. Or it wouldn't have been. But I missed my court date, and now I have to serve thirty days."

"Okay," I said slowly. I had no idea what to do. I'd wanted to have a relationship with him for years. Then, suddenly, he was standing in front of me asking for my help. I was afraid if I turned him down, I would blow my only opportunity. But still, I hesitated and floundered for something to say.

"So, why did I have to meet you out here? You could've come to the office or to the house."

"I wasn't sure if your grandparents were here. I know they don't like my mom, so I assumed they didn't care for me either."

He wasn't wrong. My grandparents despised our mother. I really didn't know how they felt about him. I'd never been allowed to see my mother; therefore, I'd never been allowed to see him. But I'd assumed that was simply because he was her son, and I wouldn't have been able to see him without seeing her.

"They're not here," I told him, instead of addressing his other requests. I was still trying to process those.

"Like I said, I'm in some trouble. I wanted it to look like I was here to check out a storage unit. Nothing more; nothing less. In case someone's watching."

"Who would be watching?"

"Blakely," he said impatiently. "Are you going to help me or not?"

I sighed. "I have no problem letting you rent a

storage unit. Will this one work?" I asked and gestured to the unit we were standing in front of.

"I don't have any money."

"Oh," I said, realizing what he was actually asking. Or so I thought.

"And I'd prefer not to have it in my name," he added.

"Why?" I asked, starting to feel uncomfortable with his request.

"I'd rather not say," he said and dropped his head. With an audible exhale, he looked up and met my eyes. "I need a unit. And I need you to take care of my son. If you're not going to help me, I need you to tell me now so I can figure out something else."

"You need me to keep him for thirty days?"

"Yes," he nodded. "Maybe a few days longer. I'm not sure if the sentence starts when I turn myself in or if they need a few days for processing."

"What about the baby's mother? Where's she?" I asked.

"I don't fucking know," he spat and started to pace the empty space. "Here I am dealing with the biggest bullshit of my life when my ex leaves me with a baby I didn't know about, says she doesn't want to be a mom, and then she fucking disappeared! I've tried to find her, but I don't have time to keep looking for her. If I don't turn myself in on time, they'll add more time to my sentence. Please, Blakely. There's no one else but you."

"What are you going to do if I say no?"

He shrugged and looked down at his son. "If you can't take him, I guess I'll have to drop him off at a police station or however you surrender a kid for foster care or whatever. That's where he'll end up if they have to come arrest me."

He had no way of knowing, but his words were the perfect ones to say to get me to agree. Because I could've easily ended up in the system. My mother decided she didn't want me not long after I was born and handed me over to my father. My father didn't want me either, so he dropped me off at my grandparents' house and never came back. Thankfully, Nana and Papa were more than willing to step up and take care of me. So, the moment he uttered the words "foster care," my decision was made. There was no way I would stand by and watch an innocent child become a ward of the state when I was fully capable of taking care of him.

"I'll do it," I said vehemently. "I'll keep him."

"Thank you," he breathed. "And don't worry. No one would think to look for him here."

My eyes widened at his words, but I managed to control my volume. "What is that supposed to mean? Who's 'no one'?"

"His mother," he clarified. "I don't know what kind of shit she was trying to pull when she dropped him off, but I've got shit going on too. So, if she changes her mind and wants to be a mother, she'll have to wait until I have my shit wrapped up to see about getting her kid back."

"What am I supposed to do if someone does come looking for him?"

"No one will," he said confidently.

"I don't like any of this," I confessed.

"You're not the only one, but it's the best plan I could come up with," he admitted. "You're really saving my ass."

I ignored his gratitude. "When do I start?"

He pressed his lips into a thin line and averted his eyes. "Tomorrow morning." His mannerisms indicated he wasn't finished, so I arched an eyebrow and waited. "Early tomorrow morning. Around three or four."

"That's not tomorrow morning!" I shouted. "That's in a few hours."

"Shhh!"

"Don't you shush me," I hissed, though I did so quietly. "What the hell, Ben? Do you have everything I'll need for him? Because I don't have anything for babies."

"Yes, I'll bring everything you'll need when I bring him over later tonight." He glanced at the time on his phone. "I need to get going. Can you make sure the gate is unlocked by three?"

"Sure," I nodded.

"Thanks again. I'll be back in a few hours."

With that, he got into his car and drove away, while I stood there staring off into the distance trying to process the past few minutes. And wondering if agreeing to help him was a huge mistake.

I'm not sure how long I had been standing in the same place when my phone buzzed in my pocket.

Landon: Are you tied up and stuffed in the trunk of a car being driven away to the gruesome death awaiting you?

Blakely: Uh, no. And that's weirdly specific. He's gone, but you can go. I'm going to check the locks on my way back.

Landon: How do I know this is you? Send me a proof of life picture.

I half sighed and half laughed at his response. Instead of snapping a selfie and sending it to him, I drove back to the front of the property.

Blakely: Look outside.

Landon appeared moments later and took the passenger's seat after locking the front door. "I'll help you check the locks if you'll give me a ride home."

I laughed and pointed to the apartment complex beside Stuff It. "You live right there."

"I know, but if I walk home, I'll be all sweaty. And you know what the humidity does to my hair," he paused and lowered his voice to a stage whisper. "I have a date tonight."

"With who?"

"This guy I matched with on a dating app…" Landon started and went on to tell me about the plans for his date while we rode through the rows of buildings to make sure each door had a secured lock in place, even the available units.

"But I don't know. What do you think?" he asked, pulling me back to the present.

"I think I wasn't listening," I admitted sheepishly.

He gave me a pointed look. "I know you weren't. What's going on?"

I shook my head and lied to my best friend. "Nothing. I didn't get much sleep last night, and I guess it's catching up with me. I'm sorry. What were you saying?" I asked and came to a stop in front of his apartment building.

"I was asking what you thought about what I'm wearing tonight, but girl, don't worry about me. Go home and get some rest. We'll talk later," he said and kissed me on the cheek.

"Have fun tonight!" I called out and blew him a kiss before I drove myself home.

Flopping down onto the couch, I tried to decide if I should stay up and wait for Ben or set an alarm to wake me in the middle of the night. Neither one sounded pleasant, but ultimately, my body made the choice for me when I fell asleep while watching videos on my phone about how to take care of babies.

* * *

Thankfully, I'd set an alarm for a quarter to three as a precaution and groaned when it woke me. I slowly rolled off the couch onto my feet and stumbled to the most used and most cherished appliance in the house—the coffee machine.

I got dressed while my coffee was being made and then took the golf cart over to Stuff It to watch for Ben from the office.

I was damn near falling asleep at the front desk

despite having finished my cup of caffeine when I finally saw a box truck drive up to the front gate. I entered the code to manually open the gate and watched as the truck drove toward unit three-seventy-three.

Inhaling deeply, I rose to my feet and went out to meet Ben, unsure of what to expect.

Ben got out of the truck with a look of surprise on his face. "What are you doing here?"

"Um, I'm here to pick up your son," I said slowly, confused by his reaction.

He scanned the area and walked to the edge of the building to peer around the side like he was looking for someone. He seemed nervous. "You should've waited."

My earlier worries of blowing my chances for a future relationship with Ben were gone. I was tired, cranky, and slightly uncomfortable with the situation, so his criticism hit a nerve. "You should've said that when you were here earlier."

"Fine, you can take him now," he huffed and walked around to the other side of the truck. Before he opened the door, he looked back at me. "One more thing, don't tell anyone he's my son."

"What? Why? What am I supposed to tell people?" I asked, not bothering to hide my shock.

He shrugged. "I don't know. Make something up. Just don't tell them the truth."

"Let me see if I've got this straight. You want me to keep him for thirty days, but I can't tell anyone that he's my nephew or why I'm watching him. How in the hell do you think I'm going to do that and work?"

"Have you ever lied before?" he shouted and threw

his hands up in frustration. "Make something up. Who's going to ask you for proof?"

"Right," I huffed. "I'll figure something out."

"I need to finish up. I don't have much time," he said and reached for a box in the back of the truck, but I stopped him.

"Oh, no. I'm not leaving yet. I still have questions that need answers," I said firmly.

"What questions?"

"What do I do if he gets sick?" I asked.

"Take him to the doctor. Next."

"Not finished with the first question. Which doctor? Does he have insurance? Am I supposed to pay for it? What about his information? Do you have his birth certificate or social security card? Or something with his full name and date of birth on it?"

"I don't fucking know!" he screamed and yanked his hair with both hands. "She didn't tell me anything when she dropped him off. I wasn't even there. She left him with some boxes and a note, so really, you know as much as I do." He exhaled slowly and dropped his hands. "I'm sorry. I don't know what to say. If something happens, I trust you to figure it out."

"Okay," I relented. "Is there some way I can contact you if something happens?"

He shook his head. "No, you can't contact me for any reason."

"What the fuck, Ben? This is your kid we're talking about here!"

"You think I don't know that?" he shouted. "It has to

be this way. I've already spent too much time here. I've gotta get going."

"Yep," I said with a nod. I wasn't happy by any means, but I knew he wasn't going to tell me more than he already had. "Can you at least write something giving me permission to have him in my care until you return?"

"I'd rather not."

I narrowed my eyes. "And I'd rather not get arrested for kidnapping. I need something saying I have permission to have him and to seek medical care if necessary, or the deal's off," I said firmly.

"Fine," he reluctantly agreed. "Do you have something I can write on?"

"I'll get something from the office," I said and returned a few minutes later with a notepad and a pen.

He handed me his sleeping son and quickly scribbled something on the piece of paper. "Here. Will that work?" he asked and thrust the paper at me.

I glanced at the note and nodded. "I guess so."

"You can take him to the house. I'll bring his stuff over as soon as I finish unloading the truck."

"Does he have a carrier or something?" I asked, looking down at the baby in my arms. "I don't have anything to put him in once I get there."

"Oh, yeah, one second," he said and opened the door to the truck. "Here you go," he said and handed me the baby's car seat.

I placed Kalen in his seat and carried him back to my house. Thirty minutes later, Ben dropped off a few boxes of baby items. "This is everything she left with him. There's also a few cans of formula and a couple of packages of diapers in one of them."

"Ben," I started. I had so many questions, and I wasn't sure which one to ask first. I didn't feel comfortable taking care of an infant around the clock for an extended period of time. At least, not without time to prepare. But Ben didn't give me the chance to voice my concerns.

"You'll be fine," he assured me and headed for the door. "I'll be back as soon as I can," he promised, and without so much as a second glance at me or his son, he left.

2

BLAKELY

The first day with Kalen was sheer and total hell. He started crying when he woke up to my unfamiliar face, and he didn't stop until he finally fell asleep an hour and a half later. No matter what I tried, nothing soothed him.

The moment he stopped crying, I started. I didn't know what to do. He kicked and screamed when I changed his wet diaper. He also peed all over me and the outfit he was wearing. He fought against me as hard as he could while I put clean clothes on him. Then, he pushed the bottle away every time I brought it to his mouth when I tried to feed him.

And there was no one I could call to ask for help. Ben wanted me to keep Kalen's presence as quiet as possible. And honestly, my options were limited anyway. I couldn't call Nana and ask for help without her wanting to know why I was asking, and I didn't want to directly lie to her. Not mentioning Kalen's presence was one thing, but outright lying to her was another. That left Landon, and I was certain he knew as much, or as little, about babies as I did. So, while Kalen napped, I looked up everything I could find online about caring for a three-month-old baby.

The rest of the day went very much like the first ninety minutes of the morning. On the plus side, the handful of customers who came into the office while Kalen was crying uncontrollably nodded sympathetically and said they'd come back another time.

Then, I did something I'd never done before and hoped I'd never have to do again. I closed the front office two hours early and went home.

I was exhausted and needed some time to regroup without worrying about ringing telephones and customers coming into the store.

When we got back to the house, I fed him a bottle, changed his diaper, and put him in his bed, hoping he was just as tired as I was. He had to be. According to the suggested schedules I'd found online, he'd missed at least one nap and hadn't slept the recommended time on the others.

Kalen slept for an hour when we got home and woke up crying. We both spent the next hour and a half in tears before he had a bottle and fell asleep. To my surprise, he slept through the night. I, on the other hand, did not. I didn't know what to expect from him, and I was afraid I wouldn't hear him if he woke up, so I spent the night tossing and turning.

I'm not sure what changed, if anything, or if the universe decided to cut me some slack, but the next day was much better. I tried my best to stick to the suggested schedule I'd found online, and it seemed to agree with Kalen. He had a few bouts of crying, but it was nothing like the day before. By the end of the second day, I felt much better about the weeks ahead.

* * *

I WAS NERVOUS ABOUT WALKING INTO THE OFFICE WITH Kalen. Landon was going to have questions that I still hadn't decided how to answer. I didn't want to lie to him, but I wanted to keep my promise to Ben.

"Excuse me. Did you have a baby over the weekend and forget to tell me?" Landon asked and followed me into my office.

"Yes, that's exactly what happened," I said flatly.

"Explain, B."

I sighed. "This is not the truth, but it's the story I'm telling if anyone asks. My friend Amanda called and asked if I could watch her son while she's out of town for work. She had somebody lined up, but they had a family emergency. Anyway, she was in a pinch, and I was able to help out, so Kalen will be around for the next few weeks," I explained while I put my things down and turned to place Kalen in the bouncy seat I set up in the office on Saturday.

"Did you say weeks?" he asked.

"Yeah," I laughed. "That was my response too."

"So," he said slowly. "What's the real story?"

"If I tell you, it might mean you have to lie to Nana and Papa. Are you okay with that?"

"I feel like that's a trick question. I don't want to lie

to them, so I wouldn't say I'm *okay* with it, but I can handle it if it's necessary," he said.

"In this instance, it's necessary."

"Understood. Now, out with it," he said and gestured for me to hurry up.

"He's my half brother Ben's son. Ben asked me to keep him while he serves thirty days in jail."

"And you said yes?" Landon asked in disbelief.

"I didn't have a choice. I mean, I could've said no, but Ben said he didn't have anyone else and that he'd end up in foster care if I couldn't help him."

Landon scoffed. "He guilted you into it."

"Pretty much," I admitted.

"What about the baby's mother? Or your mother?" he asked.

"Apparently, Kalen's mother left him on Ben's doorstep with a note saying she didn't want to be a mother anymore. I didn't ask about our mother. She didn't want to raise her own kids, so I would assume it'd be the same for her grandchildren."

"I can't believe you didn't tell me about this until now," Landon said.

"I didn't really have a chance to. It was a rough weekend," I admitted.

"Next time, call me so I can help."

"Next time?" I asked incredulously. "There better not be a next time."

"You know what I meant," he huffed. "Now, can I hold him?"

"Of course you can."

Landon clapped his hands together once and

reached down to lift Kalen from his seat. "Come here, little cutie," he cooed and cradled Kalen against his chest. "How do I look?" he asked and struck a pose.

"You look good with a baby," I said sincerely.

"Thanks!" he beamed. "Oh, before I forget, something's wrong with the security cameras. When I checked the app, it said the cameras were offline and have been since around six o'clock Friday evening. I'm not sure how we missed it before we closed. I did everything listed in the troubleshooting section, but nothing worked. Do you want me to call and see if someone needs to come out?" he asked and handed the baby back to me when he started to fuss.

"Yes, thank you," I said and placed Kalen in his bouncy seat. "I'll be in here for a while. This little guy wasn't such a happy camper on Saturday, so I have some paperwork to catch up on."

"I'll give Jackson Security a call now," he said and went back to the front desk.

Landon knocked on my door and pushed it open a few minutes later. "The earliest Jackson Security can have someone here is Sunday. The next available appointment after that is the following Saturday."

I didn't like the thought of not having working security cameras for almost two weeks, especially while I was taking care of Kalen. I couldn't put my finger on it, but something about the situation with Ben wasn't sitting right with me. I'd felt uneasy since he'd left his son with me. So, I opted for the first available appointment even though the office was closed on Sundays.

I'd already been thinking about adding on to our security system since several cars had been broken into at the apartment complex where Landon lived, which was right beside Stuff It. But when I realized the cameras stopped working the same night Ben showed up with Kalen, I decided to go ahead and have the security system upgraded when they came out to replace or repair the cameras.

3

BLAKELY

"Hello," a male voice called from the front of the store. "I'm here with Jackson Security."

I grabbed my cell phone from my desk and quickly closed the door to my office. "Sorry about that," I started and turned around to introduce myself. But I damn near choked on my tongue when my eyes landed on the man standing in front of me. Dark blonde hair. Blue eyes. Muscles. Tattoos. I knew I was staring, but I couldn't even make myself blink.

And then he grinned.

"Hi," he extended his hand. "I'm Grant. Are you Blakely?"

I shook his hand, intending to answer, but fell silent when his tattooed fingers brushed the skin on my wrist. Clearing my throat, I nodded, "Yes, that's me."

"Great. If I can have a few minutes of your time to go over everything with you, I'll get out of your way."

"Of course," I smiled. But I didn't want him to get out of my way. In fact, he could've stood directly in front of me all day, and I wouldn't have minded one bit. Especially if he smelled as good as he looked.

"Is that correct?" he asked, bringing my attention back to the present.

Shit. Was what correct? I had no idea what he was talking about because I was too busy drooling over every delicious inch of him. "Uh, repair or replace the cameras that aren't working, add two more, and add sensors to all entry points for the office," I said, repeating what should have been on the work order.

He nodded in response. "Yes, that's what I have here. I'll start outside with the cameras and finish with the sensors in the office," he said and turned toward the door.

"Thank you," I smiled and, for some unknown reason, waved before I spun on my heel and disappeared into my office.

What in the hell was wrong with me? He was the first attractive guy I'd seen in months, and what did I do? I waved like a five-year-old. No matter how hard I tried, whenever I was nervous, I always did something completely embarrassing. Instead of being blessed with grace or elegance, I was the queen of clumsy and awkward.

Thankfully, we were closed on Sundays, so I was able to hide out in my office for the majority of the time he was there. However, that also meant I didn't have much to do, especially during Kalen's nap times.

When he went down for his second nap of the day, I decided to be a diligent manager and opened the blinds to keep an eye on Grant while he worked around the property.

I'd been watching him with rapt attention for a while when he wiped the sweat from his forehead and squinted up at the sun. Keeping my eyes fixed on the window, I wanted to squeal in delight when he sat back on his heels and looked around before he gripped the hem of his polo and ripped it off over his head.

"Hot fucking damn," I breathed and rolled my chair closer to the window while I shamelessly stared at him. I'd never seen a body like his—chiseled abs, sculpted shoulders, and biceps bigger than my thighs. At least, not in person, and I wasn't going to miss my chance to get a better view.

After a quick glance at my phone to check the temperature outside, I couldn't stop myself. I was pretty sure he had water, but nothing, and I mean absolutely nothing, was better at quenching your thirst and cooling you down than a glass of ice-cold lemonade. Since I'd made a fresh pitcher that morning, I poured a glass for him, picked up the baby monitor, and headed out the door after checking on Kalen.

Grant reached for his shirt the moment he spotted me walking toward him. "Sorry, it—"

I waved my hand dismissively. "It's hot." Then, I held up the glass. "Thirsty?"

He wiped the sweat from his face with a black bandana and tucked it into his back pocket before he climbed down the ladder. "Yes, ma'am," he said and reached for the lemonade. "Thank you."

"Did you just ma'am me?"

"Depends," he winked. "Was I supposed to?"

I laughed. "Good answer."

Once again, I blatantly watched as he brought the drink to his full lips and proceeded to drain the remainder of the contents in one go. I couldn't decide if I wanted to be the glass or the lemonade.

He pointed the glass in my direction when he finished and met my eyes. "This is the best lemonade I've ever had," he said seriously.

A thrill of excitement shot through me. "Would you like a refill?"

He ran his fingers over his chin. "We're technically not supposed to accept things from customers, but that was too good to turn down."

"I won't tell if you won't," I grinned. "I'll be right back."

I returned a few minutes later with an insulated tumbler full of lemonade for him. "Here you go. This should keep it cold while you're working."

"Thank you," he grinned and took a sip. "So fu—, uh, good."

That grin was going to be trouble. Every tingle in my body said so.

"Thanks. I'm glad you like it."

His grin turned into a full-on smile. "Me too."

I was wrong. So wrong. His grin was child's play. His smile was what was going to steal my heart. His smile and his piercing blue eyes.

I floundered for something else to say and came up empty. Awkwardly swinging my arms, I said, "Well, I'll let you get back to it." With that, I headed back to the office and hoped my ass looked good if he was checking it out as I walked away.

* * *

To my utter disappointment, Grant put his shirt on before he came inside to install the entry point sensors in the office.

"We have three doors and two windows down for sensors on the work order. Does that sound correct?" he asked.

"Yes," I confirmed. "Front door, back door, side door, and those two windows," I said and pointed to each location as I mentioned it.

He pointed to the front. "I'll get the sensors from the truck and work my way around to each one."

While he was outside, I stepped into my office to check on Kalen, who was still napping in his seat. Quietly closing the door, I returned to the front and took a seat behind the counter before Grant came back inside.

When he returned, he didn't acknowledge me until he finished with the first sensor. "Hi," I waved, before quickly putting my hand down and shoving it underneath my thigh.

He chuckled. "Hey."

"So, about this lemonade," he said as he moved to one of the windows. "Did you make it?"

"I did," I said proudly.

"What do you do to make it taste so good?"

"I can't tell you; it's a secret recipe," I teased.

He turned back to me with a serious expression on his face. "Well, if you're not going to tell me, are you gonna make some more for me?"

I didn't know how to respond. I thought he was joking, but I wasn't sure. Before I could formulate a response, his phone rang.

He glanced at the screen. "Excuse me. I need to take this," he said and stepped outside to answer the call.

After his phone call, he resumed installing the sensors while I pretended to work and tried to think of something to say to fill the awkward silence.

"Did you find out why the cameras weren't working?" I finally asked.

"Yes, a wire was severed. I can't say for sure if it was caused by an animal or something else, but after I replaced the damaged wire, both cameras came back online."

"So, you didn't have to replace either one of them?"

"Nope. Just the wire."

Since I didn't have to pay for two new cameras, I wondered if that would leave me with enough money to add a basic alarm system to the house. Even though Ben had assured me not to worry, I'd been on edge since his unexpected visit and subsequent requests, especially when I was at home at night.

4

GAME

"How much does a basic residential system cost?" she asked. "Like a camera and a few door sensors for a house or whatever comes with the cheapest package you have."

She attempted to sound casual, but something in her tone caught my attention. I'd heard the sound of underlying fear many times and recognized it easily. But never before had it made me feel the need to intervene.

I wanted to tell her she didn't need to waste her money on a security system because all she had to do was give me the motherfucker's name, and I'd take care of him for her. Instead, I tamped down my personal feelings and answered professionally. "I don't know off the top of my head, but I'll be happy to call and get a quote for you." I glanced at my phone to check the time. "No pressure, but if you do want to add a system to your house, we had a cancellation, so I can probably install it today."

"Really?" she asked hopefully.

And that was all it took. When the worry and fear on her beautiful face disappeared, coupled with the sound of relief in her voice, the decision was made for me. I didn't care what price Judge quoted; she was getting a system put into her house even if I had to pay for it myself.

"Hey, man. Everything going okay?" Judge asked.

"Yeah. I just finished the job at Stuff It, and the customer asked for a price quote for a home install," I said and told him what features she wanted.

Judge chuckled. "So, why do you need me? You know the prices for basic installs."

"She asked for the cheapest one we have, so I'm guessing she's on a tight budget, and I wanted to see if there was anything we could do to help her out."

"Give me a second to pull up her account."

"She's scared," I blurted.

"Yeah," he said knowingly. "Most of my customers are. At least in the beginning."

"I know," I paused and exhaled slowly. "But this is different."

"How so?"

"I'm not sure," I admitted. "It's just a feeling, but I don't think I should ignore it."

"Gotcha. So, yeah, they've been loyal customers for a few years. Let me see," he trailed off. "Looks like I've got two cameras—one is refurbished, and the other one was never used, but I'm not going to use it for new installs because the newer model was released last month. She can have both cameras, as well as the sensors, free of charge."

"So, she'd just be responsible for the monthly fee?"

"Yes, and we can give her a fifty percent discount on the monthly service since she has a business account in good standing with us."

"Thanks, brother. If she decides to go ahead with it, I'll do the installation this afternoon. Off the clock."

Judge laughed. "Can't say I didn't see that coming."

"Yep. Appreciate it." Completely ignoring his remark, I ended the call and went back inside.

"I spoke with the owner," I started and told her about the fifty percent discount before I went over the regular prices for basic home installations. "But, if you're interested in saving some money, we have two previously owned cameras that can be installed for free."

"Do the free cameras come with the special rate?" she asked hopefully.

"Yes. Regardless of which option you choose, you still get the monthly discount."

"And there's nothing wrong with the used equipment?"

"No. Technically, one has never been used, but we're now installing the newer model that was released last month. The other one is refurbished and comes with a one-year warranty. If it stops working, we'll repair it or replace it for free," I added, knowing the cost would come out of my pocket if the camera crapped out on her.

She clapped her hands together once. "I'll take the free cameras, one-year guarantee, and discounted plan, please."

I wanted to smile, and possibly pump my fist, but I

managed to contain myself. "Great. Do you want me to install the system today?"

"Do you have time? I don't want to mess up someone else's appointment."

I couldn't tell her I was working for free because she struck some deep-seated protective instinct in me with her worry-filled eyes and her damn lemonade. "I do. They blocked my whole day for this job and the one that was just canceled."

"What would you do for the rest of the day if I hadn't opted for an additional security system?"

I chuckled. "I wouldn't be getting off early if that's what you're worried about. I'll be working until five o'clock today one way or another." Though I probably would have been working at the gym instead of helping Judge get caught up.

"As long as I'm not inconveniencing you, or someone else."

"Not at all," I reassured her. "I'll take my lunch break now and stop by the office to pick up the cameras. I should be back in an hour or so."

"Sounds good," she smiled and raised her hand like she was going to wave again but quickly dropped it.

* * *

A LITTLE OVER AN HOUR LATER, I WAS STANDING IN front of her house waiting for her to answer the door. I didn't see a doorbell, so I knocked. And then knocked again a few minutes later.

Nothing. No sound was coming from the house, and

it didn't seem like anyone was home. But she knew I was coming back.

I walked back to the van to get her phone number from the work order so I could call and let her know I was at her house.

"Hello?" she answered.

"Hey, Blakely, it's Grant with Jackson Security."

"Oh, hey. Is something wrong?"

"Well, I'm here, and you're not."

"What?" she asked, followed by the sound of a door opening. "Where?"

"At your house."

I heard Blakely's laughter in stereo moments later and turned to see her rounding the corner of the house. "Sorry, I forgot to tell you to come to the side door. That one's only for strangers and solicitors," she said and pointed to the front door.

"Why's that?" I asked.

"Because Papa sealed it shut and put up a wall on the other side of it. He left the door there for the people he didn't want to see. He said all the people he cared about knew to use the side door, and everyone else could piss off."

"Your Papa sounds like a smart man."

"One of the smartest," she said proudly.

"Do you know where you would like your cameras?"

"Sort of. With the new additions, the cameras from Stuff It cover most of the front yard," she explained. "I want the other two to cover as much of the back and side yards as possible, but I'm not sure of the best way to achieve that."

"I'll take a look when I get back there. I may not be able to get the entire area covered with two cameras, but I should be able to get most of it."

"Sounds good. I'll be inside if you need anything."

With that, she disappeared into the house while I wondered what in the hell was wrong with me. Well, I knew what was wrong with me, but I wasn't ready to admit it.

So, I ignored the way my heart raced at the thought of her, the way my stomach flipped at the sound of her voice, and the way my eyes followed every move she made.

Falling head over dick for a chick was not on my immediate agenda. Most of my time was occupied by the gym and the club. I had no complaints about the way my life was going, and therefore, saw no reason to change it.

I lightly tapped on the screen door to get Blakely's attention. "All finished."

She turned off the water at the sink and gestured for me to come in while she dried her hands.

I quickly went over the new equipment with her since she was already familiar with the cameras and sensors at her business. "Do you have any questions?"

"No, I don't think so."

Damn. I was hoping she did. Because I wasn't ready to leave.

I smiled tightly to cover my misplaced disappointment. "Give us a call at the office if you have any problems."

"I will. Thank you again for everything," she said sincerely.

"You're welcome. Enjoy the rest of your day."

"Oh, I almost forgot." She darted back to the kitchen and returned with a gallon of lemonade. "I made this for you."

She was too fucking sweet, and it was killing me. I'd had to constantly remind myself that I was there as a Jackson Security employee to do a job, when all I really wanted to do was pin her to the wall and devour every inch of her. And despite how much I didn't want to admit it, I wanted to talk to her. To get to know her. And then she went and made me lemonade.

5

BLAKELY

After a few days of keeping Kalen, I learned it was better if I waited until after he went down for the night before I took a shower and had dinner. It worked out well since I liked to eat later than most, and he liked to cry whenever I was eating.

And since I had one of my favorite meals in the oven, I wanted to sit down and enjoy it. It'd been a rough week, and I deserved it.

I was still in the bathroom drying off from my shower when my phone buzzed on the counter with a text from a number that looked vaguely familiar but wasn't saved in my phone.

Unknown Number: Hey. This is Grant with Jackson Security. Did I leave my tablet there?

When I walked out to the kitchen and immediately spotted it on the counter, I wondered how I hadn't noticed it before.

Blakely: Yes, you did.

Grant: Sorry about that. Can I come pick it up?

I looked down at the tank top and leggings I had planned to wear for dinner and had a minor moment of panic.

Blakely: Can you give me about thirty minutes?

Grant: I'm at your mercy. I'll make any time work.

Blakely: Okay. See you then.

Grant: Thank you.

I set a timer for twenty-five minutes and ran to my bedroom to find something to wear. I had no idea how long it would take Grant to get to my house, and I couldn't answer the door in what I currently had on.

I wanted to shout with glee when I saw my laundry basket full of clean clothes sitting on top of my bed. "Score one for me for being somewhat of an adult."

Once I was dressed, I returned to the bathroom to do something with my hair and face. I didn't want to put makeup on since I'd just showered, but I at least needed to make sure I didn't have any leftover mascara under my eyes or after-shower boogers in my nose.

I checked my phone and smiled gleefully. There was enough time for me to dry my hair and have a few minutes left over. Or so I thought.

I jumped when my alarm went off, and almost busted my ass when my socked feet hit the tile floor, and I lost my balance.

With my heart racing, I tiptoed across the hall to check on Kalen and make sure the door to his room was securely closed. I didn't know if the doorbell would be loud enough to wake him, and I didn't want to take the chance. Then, I hurried to the kitchen to wait by the side door and watch for Grant.

I was startled once again when the timer on the oven went off, and I laughed at myself for being so jumpy. I swapped the pans and reset the timer before resuming my perch by the door.

Even though I was expecting him, a jolt of anxiety shot through me when headlights I didn't recognize turned into my driveway. Then, I breathed a sigh of relief when Grant got out of the driver's side moments later.

I was about to step outside and take the tablet to him when the timer on the oven beeped.

Letting go of the screen door, I darted back to the kitchen to silence the blaring noise before it woke the sleeping baby. I never realized how loud everyday noises were until I had an infant in the house.

"Knock, knock," he called out as he tapped on the screen door's metal frame.

"Sorry. The timer just went off," I said as I carefully removed the bread and placed it on top of the stove. "Come on in. Your tablet is right there on the island."

I heard the door open and close, followed by the sound of his approaching footsteps.

I turned in time to see him inhale deeply and briefly close his eyes. "Mmm. Something smells delicious."

"Thanks. It's lasagna and garlic bread. Would you like some?" I offered.

"Oh, no, I couldn't impose," he said reluctantly.

"You sure? It's so hard to make decent meals for one person. It'll go to waste before I can finish it," I added, hoping he'd cave.

"You're making me break a lot of rules today," he groaned.

"What rules?"

He shook his head and chuckled. "Fraternizing with customers for one."

"Technically, you're off work, so I'm not your customer," I countered.

He nodded in agreement. "I like the way you think. Is there anything I can do to help?"

"Nope," I said and gestured to the table. "Make yourself comfortable."

While he took a seat, I followed him to the table with two plates loaded with lasagna. "What would you like to drink?"

He gave me a pointed look. "Really?"

"I didn't want to assume," I laughed and filled two glasses with lemonade before joining him at the table.

"I will never say no to your lemonade," he admitted and shoved a forkful of food into his mouth. "And this," he groaned. "Holy shit, this is good."

I beamed proudly. "Thank you. It's my Nana's recipe."

"You got any more of her recipes?" he asked and

continued to shovel food into his mouth. He was almost halfway finished before I even had two bites of mine.

I pointed to Nana's special recipe book on the counter. "There are two more books full of her recipes in the cabinet. Nana loves to cook."

"I'm guessing you do too?"

"I do."

"Did she teach you?"

"Yes," I answered proudly. "She started teaching me when I was little. Even after all these years, I still learn something new from her every time we get to cook together."

"Is that often?" he asked, keeping the conversation flowing. And he seemed genuinely interested in my answers.

"A few times a year. Usually when they come home for holidays or birthdays."

"Where are they when they're not home?"

"Traveling. They bought an RV and are fulfilling their retirement dreams," I smiled wistfully.

"Sounds like you miss them," he observed.

"I do, but at the same time, I'm so happy they're gone." I immediately cringed and covered my face with my palm. "Oh, that sounded bad. That's not what I meant."

He laughed while I hurried to explain.

"Papa got sick a few years ago, and things weren't looking good for a little while, but he pulled through. When he was up and at it again, Nana said she wasn't wasting the second chance they'd been given. Within a month's time, they bought an RV and hit the road."

"Your grandparents sound like pretty awesome people."

"They are." I wiped my mouth with a napkin and leaned back in my chair, glancing at his clean plate. "Did you save room for dessert?"

"If you made it, yes," he grinned.

"I did," I smiled and got to my feet. "You don't want to know what it is first?"

He placed his elbows on the table and leaned forward. "I'm going to be completely honest with you," he said seriously. "I have a sweet tooth. I have yet to find a dessert I don't like."

"I think we're going to be friends," I said with a sly smile and went to the kitchen.

I returned with the dessert I made the night before, hoping I didn't screw it up. "Fair warning, I've never made tiramisu before, so eat it at your own risk."

He looked from the plate to me. "When's the last time you messed up a recipe?"

"Hmm." I tried to think of the last time and couldn't. "I don't remember," I laughed.

"Then I'll take my chances," he said and brought the first bite to his lips. I watched with rapt attention as his lips wrapped around the spoon before he slowly slid it from his mouth.

He closed his eyes and groaned, which thankfully was loud enough to cover the slight whimper from me.

Realizing my mouth was gaping open, I slammed it shut just as he opened his eyes and pointed the spoon at me. "You most certainly did not screw this up."

I exhaled in relief—for not messing up the dessert as

well as for not being caught gawking. Then, I brought my own spoon to my mouth to see if it really did turn out okay or if he was just being polite.

Grant laughed. "I wasn't just saying that."

"I had to check," I shrugged. "But I'm glad you like it."

"I do," he paused and met my eyes. "Just like everything else you've put in front of me today."

Holy. Shit.

He couldn't mean me. Could he? No, he had to be talking about the food.

One corner of his lips turned up in a half smile, as if he knew what I was thinking, before he turned his attention back to the plate and finished his dessert.

I carried our plates and silverware to the sink and turned to get the glasses, but Grant was already bringing them to me.

"Thank you," I smiled and put them in the sink. "I'll get the rest later."

"I can't let you do that," he said seriously.

"And why is that?" I asked, hoping I sounded confident because I wasn't sure what to make of his sudden change in demeanor.

"The one who cooks doesn't clean up after the meal," he said and gently ushered me away from the sink.

I watched in disbelief as he started to rinse the dishes and load the dishwasher. After a few moments of shamelessly staring, I put some of the food into containers for Grant to take home.

When he was finished, I walked him to the door.

"Thank you for dinner. It was hands down one of the best meals of my life."

"You're welcome." I extended my hand with the bag of leftovers. "Here's some for you to take home."

He took the bag from my hand and placed it on the table by the door. "You're too fucking sweet," he said and wrapped his hand around the back of my neck before he covered my mouth with his.

And I was gone. Lost in the moment. His hands. His lips. His body. His warmth. His everything.

Far too soon, he broke the kiss and rested his forehead against the top of my head. "We doing this again?"

"We can."

"When?"

"Wednesday?" I suggested.

"I'll be here," he said and used his hands to tilt my head back.

My eyes locked with his, and my stomach quivered. I licked my lips. "I can't wait."

"Fuck," he muttered. In a flash, he hoisted me up by my ass, causing my legs to involuntarily wrap around his waist, only because my voluntary reflexes weren't fast enough. Then, his large body was pressing mine against the wall while our mouths fused together.

When he pulled back, I tightened my fingers in his hair, trying to keep him where he was. He smiled against my lips. "I don't want to stop. And I damn sure don't want to leave, but I'm going to fuck you against this wall in a matter of minutes if I don't go."

"Okay," I said quietly, relieved and disappointed at the same time.

He dropped his mouth to my ear and whispered, "I'm going to fuck you, sweets. But I'm going to behave tonight."

Well, I wasn't. As soon as he left, I all but sprinted to my bedroom and used my vibrator to finish what he started.

6

GAME

I should have never stepped into the ring, but in my defense, I didn't realize how distracted I was until it was too late. Too late as in a fraction of a second before Trent's fist crashed into my face.

"Fuck," I mumbled behind my mouth guard as I stumbled back a few steps.

"Told ya, motherfucker!" Judge shouted.

Bronze shook his head and laughed. Then, he pointed a finger at Batta. "You owe me twenty bucks."

"Fuck all of y'all," I laughed and stuck both middle fingers in the air when *Pussy Whipped Again* began to play through the speakers.

"Where are you going?" Batta asked when I climbed out of the ring.

"To put ice on my eye," I said simply without breaking my stride.

Bronze clapped his hands together and laughed. "He must have a date tonight."

"Yeah, I do. And I don't want to be late because

she's cooking dinner for me again," I paused and looked directly at Bronze. "With dessert. Made from scratch."

"You should bring her to the party this weekend," he suggested.

I snorted. "If I do, she's not bringing anything for you."

"Oh, come on," he pouted. "At least sneak me some leftovers. Sloane's coming up on a deadline, and Leigh's been 'busy.'"

"Learn to make your own sweets," I suggested.

"He already knows how," Batta laughed and nudged Bronze with his elbow. "Tell him why you don't make your own cookies and shit."

Bronze straightened and lifted his chin. "When I make them, they don't taste as good as they do when they were made by someone else." Then, he turned to Batta and said something I couldn't hear.

I could still hear them laughing and cutting up while I jogged up the stairs to my office. Normally, I would have washed off in the locker room before leaving, but I wanted to shower at home before I went over to Blakely's for dinner. But first, I stopped by the cold therapy room to get some ice and pressed it against the side of my face. Even though it stung, I held it there because I could already tell it was going to look like hell and I wanted to lessen it as much as I could.

Since I couldn't ride and hold the ice to my face, I went to my office, planning to take a quick cat nap on the sofa. However, my plans quickly changed when I realized someone had been in my office. The top of my desk was a mess and several of the drawers weren't completely closed.

I stepped out into the hall and called for Drew. Then, I stuck my head in the other two offices and found them to be in the same state as mine.

"Did you need something?" Drew asked.

"Yeah. Somebody's been in the offices. Have you seen anyone down this way?" I asked and headed back to my office to look at the camera feed.

"No, I haven't," he said and followed me inside. "What the hell?" he asked when he saw the mess they left behind.

"Coal's office is the same way. Savior's too."

"Is anything missing?" he asked.

"I'm not sure. I haven't had a chance to look yet. Will you ask Coal and Savior to come up here? They're both downstairs."

"Sure, man. Be right back."

While he was gone, I started reviewing the camera feed. It didn't take me long to find what I was looking for. About twenty minutes before I came upstairs, someone went into each of the offices, spending a few minutes in each one. I couldn't tell if the person was male or female by the way they were dressed—sweatshirt, sweatpants, and a baseball hat.

When Coal and Savior arrived, I showed them the footage.

"Did they take anything?" Coal asked.

"Not from what I can tell," I said.

"Why would someone rummage through our offices and not take anything?" Savior asked.

"I have no idea. What could they possibly have been looking for? We don't keep anything worth stealing in the offices," I said.

"Do either of you recognize them as one of our gym members?" Coal asked.

Savior squinted at the screen. "It's hard to tell. I don't think they wanted to be recognized."

"I think you're right," I agreed.

"Guess we need to start locking the doors," Coal suggested.

"Yeah, and I'll print out a still frame to put at the front desk so they can keep an eye out," I said.

"I'll let the guys downstairs know if you want to head out," Savior said.

I clapped his shoulder. "Thanks, man. Pretty sure I'm going to be late. Let me know if you figure out who it was."

"Will do. Enjoy your evening."

I looked at the time and grimaced. I was definitely going to be late, so I sent Blakely a text to let her know.

Grant: Something came up at work. Okay if I'm thirty minutes late?

Blakely: No rush. Later works better for me too.

Grant: Need me to bring anything?

Blakely: Just your appetite.

Grinning, I put my phone in my pocket and went

home to shower and change clothes. Since my face was sore and I had a slight headache, I opted to take my truck instead of my bike.

When I arrived, I made sure to keep my head down while I walked to the door because I didn't want her to see my black eye before I had a chance to warn her about it. But I wasn't expecting her to be waiting by the door for me.

I was startled when she pushed the screen door open. "Hey."

My head shot up as a natural response, giving her a perfect view of my bruised eye and swollen cheek. It wasn't bad, but it was noticeable.

"Are you okay?" she gasped and reached for my face but stopped before she made contact. "What happened?"

I closed the distance between us and gently turned her around to usher her inside. "I'm fine," I assured. "I got tagged when I was sparring at the gym. Probably looks worse than it is."

"It doesn't look great," she said and glanced over her shoulder as we walked into the house. "Have a seat," she waved at the table. "I have something for that."

She returned with a bag of frozen peas. "This should help."

I circled her wrist and tugged her into my lap. "You always this sweet?"

"Yes," she nodded once. "Until you piss me off."

"I'll try to avoid doing that," I said and leaned forward, quickly kissing her lips, and immediately going back for more.

"We should have dinner before it gets cold," she said softly.

I followed her into the kitchen and wanted to pump my fist when my eyes landed on fried chicken, green beans, mashed potatoes, and peach cobbler. "Plates and silverware are on the counter," she said and turned to get our drinks.

I grinned when I saw her pouring two glasses of lemonade out of the corner of my eye.

"Do you spar often?" she asked once we were seated at the table.

"Almost every day," I replied. "I'm one of the managers at Pumpers, the gym downtown. We have a training program for fighters, and I spar with at least one of them whenever I work."

"I thought you worked for Jackson Security," she said carefully.

"I do and I don't. My full-time job is at the gym. My brother owns Jackson Security, and he asked me to help him get caught up."

"That was nice of you. How many brothers and sisters do you have?"

I wiped my mouth with my napkin. "Well, I have one sister, but that's not what I meant," I paused and waited until I had her eyes. "I was talking about my club brother. I'm a member of the Blackwings MC."

I wasn't sure what kind of reaction to expect from her, so I took a large bite of the delicious fried chicken in case she kicked me out.

She watched me curiously and laughed. "I'm not

scared of the bikers in town. Actually, I have a funny story about one of the Blackwings."

"I'd love to hear it," I told her, not bothering to mask the tremendous amount of relief I felt when she didn't seem to care one way or the other about my affiliation with the club.

"One time, when I was seven or eight, Nana left her lights on while we were in the grocery store. While she was trying to figure out why her car wouldn't start, a man came over to help us. He gave me a sucker before he jump-started her car. He was really nice, and we were on our way home in a few minutes. But before we went inside the house, she told me not to tell Papa what happened. I didn't understand why but said okay. So, we went inside, and Papa asked me where I got the sucker. I said, 'From the nice big man in leather that Nana jacked off,' and continued on my way to the back yard to play."

"You didn't?" I laughed.

"I did, but in my defense, I didn't say anything about Nana leaving her lights on. However, she did have to tell him when she explained what really happened after my little mix-up."

"Do you know why she didn't want to tell him?" I asked carefully.

"Yeah, I do. Papa said Nana was bad about leaving the lights on. She insisted she wasn't. The last time it happened, Papa said he'd bet fifty dollars that she'd do it again within six months. They shook on it, and two months later, she was 'jacked off' by a Blackwing."

"How long ago was that?"

"Probably seventeen or eighteen years ago, I think," she said.

"I wonder who it was. Do you remember his name?"

"No, I'm not sure I ever knew his name."

"Damn. Do you think you'd recognize him if you saw him?" I asked.

She shrugged. "Depends on how much he's changed. But I'm sure I'd recognize a picture of him from back then."

"You'll have to come by the clubhouse and look at some of the pictures. Actually, we're having a party Saturday night. Would you like to come?"

When she looked down at her plate, I cursed myself for asking too soon. Instead of backpedaling, I waited to see what she'd say.

"I'd love to, but I'm keeping my friend's three-month-old son."

"Bring him with you."

"To a party at your clubhouse?" she asked incredulously.

I nodded. "Several of the members have kids, so the clubhouse is family friendly. At least before dark. Even then, it's probably nowhere near what you're imagining."

"I was picturing a dark, smoke-filled room with heavy metal music blasting through the speakers," she admitted.

"Nah, Copper's never allowed any smoking inside the clubhouse, but the music can get loud. A while back, when we converted one of the bedrooms to a nursery and playroom for the kids, we soundproofed the room and wired it with cameras. Which was sort of a waste of money because there's almost always at least one adult in the room when kids are there."

"How old are the kids?"

"The oldest is Riley. She's around ten years old. And the youngest is Blue, who's almost a year old. Braxton is seven years old, Sienna will be two in November, and Brinkley is four years old. Those are the club kids, but somehow, we always end up with other children."

"Let me talk to my friend. If she doesn't have a problem with it, we'd love to come."

"There is one thing I should mention. The reason we're having the party is to watch an MMA fight. A few of the club members are related to one of the fighters. He's actually fighting in the main event, so it'll be pretty late when his match starts. If you do come and stay for the fight, you're welcome to spend the night in one of the guest rooms," I offered.

"How late are we talking?"

"The main event will probably start sometime between eleven and midnight."

"Yeah, that is kind of late," she said but didn't give any indication one way or the other what she thought about spending the night.

"Most of the brothers and their families end up staying at the clubhouse after one of Nathan's fights. And like I said, we have a few guest rooms, so you and the baby would have your own room. You're welcome to stay in my room, but I wanted you to know there are other options if you're not comfortable with that," I explained.

"So, if we did stay, you'd be there?" she asked.

"Of course. I wouldn't leave you there," I said.

"Just checking," she grinned. "I'll give my friend a call in the morning. Can I let you know sometime tomorrow?" she asked.

I nodded. "There's no rush. You could let me know the day of and it'd be fine."

"Great," she smiled. "I don't think she'll have a problem with it, but I need to make sure."

7

BLAKELY

"Keep smiling like that and you're going to have some hellacious lines on your face when you're older," Landon said the moment he walked through the door the next day.

"Good. Deep smile lines indicate a happy life," I quipped.

"Not if you've got a good plastic surgeon," he teased and stopped by his desk before he headed to the break room.

I followed behind him. "I was up late with the baby last night."

He rolled his eyes. "The baby might be the reason for your tired eyes, but he's not behind the smile." He lowered his voice and asked, "Did you get a new vibrator?"

"What? No," I blurted and doubled over laughing.

"You want a cup of coffee while you tell me about your mystery man?"

"How did you know about him?" I gasped. "And yes. When have I ever said no to coffee?"

"It was only a guess, but your response confirmed it." I could hear the laughter in his voice.

He filled two mugs with coffee and handed one to me before we returned to the front desk. "All right, tell me everything. And by everything, I mean only the good stuff. Save all the boring details for your diary." He sipped his coffee and stared at me while he waited for me to share.

I sighed with mock exasperation. "Okay, fine. I met a guy and we've had dinner twice."

"I knew it! Where'd you meet him?" Landon asked excitedly.

"Um, he was the guy from Jackson Security who came out to fix the cameras."

"What else did he fix?" he asked suggestively.

"Nothing like that," I giggled. "I ended up getting an alarm system for the house too. He left his tablet on the kitchen counter, and I was cooking when he came back to get it. He ended up staying for dinner."

"How did that turn into two dinners?"

"He said he liked my cooking, so I invited him to dinner again."

Landon waggled his eyebrows. "I bet that's not all he likes."

"One can only hope."

"I swear, it's like pulling teeth with you. What's his name? How old is he? What does he look like?" he paused and gasped dramatically. "Pull up the security feed from Sunday so I can see him."

I reached for my phone and brought up the footage from the day of the install. I hadn't gone back to look at anything other than the alarm trigger alerts sent to my phone. So, I had no idea that one of the cameras caught the majority of Grant working his ass off completely shirtless.

Landon yanked my phone from my hands and brought it close to his face. "Girl! Are you serious, right now? Look at him! Shit, all he has to do is stand there to put a smile on your face. Mmm-hmm. I'm going to be honest. I'm a little jealous. In the non-bitchy way. You know, happy for you, but I want to be happy too."

I placed my hand on his shoulder and gently squeezed. "You will be," I assured. Landon was a great guy and had a lot to offer. He was going to make someone very happy one day.

He sighed and put all humor aside. "It's hard to believe that with my track record."

"Your track record is exactly what it's supposed to be," I pointed out. "Every relationship you have is going to end, and likely end badly, until you find the right one."

"You're probably not wrong," he reluctantly admitted.

"If I thought I was wrong, I wouldn't have said anything," I laughed. "It creates the illusion of always being right."

"That's brilliant!" he gasped. "Teach me your ways, oh wise one."

"All in due time. Besides, I thought things were going well with the new guy. Did something change?"

"They are. We've been on two dates, but it's still early. I'm trying not to get my hopes up," he said.

Landon's gaze went back to the screen. "Oh, what do we have here? You little hussy. Look at you prancing out there with a glass of lemonade for him."

I snatched my phone back. "You saw nothing."

"Don't keep me waiting. When are you seeing him again?" he prodded.

"He's a member of the Blackwings MC, and he invited me to a party at their clubhouse this weekend."

"Are you going to go?"

"I don't know. When I told him I was babysitting for my friend, he told me to bring the baby. He said they have a designated room for the kids. I do want to go, but I'm not sure I should bring Kalen with me," I admitted. "What do you think?"

"I don't think you should run around doing whatever you want without any regard for Kalen's safety and well-being, but I also don't think you should put your life on hold while you're keeping him. Four weeks is a long time. You're doing your 'friend' a favor, without any notice, and you're not being paid. But if you're truly not sure, and you want to go, maybe Kalen could spend the night with your best friend while you go get you some biker booty," Landon suggested.

"But I already told Grant I was babysitting this weekend."

"So, tell him your friend called and plans changed. He doesn't need to know why," he said simply.

"You make everything seem so easy."

"Everything is easy when you don't overthink it."

I raised my hand in the air. "Guilty as charged."

"I know. Go on in your office and overthink our conversation. Make a list or whatever you need to do, and we'll talk about it on our next break."

* * *

LANDON KNOCKED ON MY DOOR A FEW HOURS LATER. "I'm getting ready to leave for my doctor's appointment."

"Crap. I completely forgot about that," I admitted. "Go ahead and go. I'll be right out there."

"All right. I'll see you tomorrow."

I moved Kalen and his bouncy seat to the area behind the front desk and made myself comfortable in Landon's usual spot. The afternoon was relatively quiet, so I was able to finish sending out late notices while keeping Kalen entertained.

I was just about to start my closing routine when a customer came through the front door.

"Hi, can I help you?" I asked with a smile.

"Yes, I wanted to talk to someone about renting a unit here," he said.

"I'm sorry, we don't have any units available right now, but I can add you to our waiting list if you'd like."

"That's okay. I don't need one immediately. I'm still shopping around. How much are your units?" he asked.

"It depends on the size you want, but here's our price list," I said and handed him a printout.

He took it and nodded without so much as glancing

at the information before shoving it into his back pocket. "What kind of security do you have?"

"The property is surrounded by a fence with a locked gate. Each renter is given a unique code to access the property. We also have twenty-four-hour surveillance with security cameras," I explained.

"So, you don't have someone here all the time?"

"No, we don't have a caretaker who lives on site, but the owner does live close by." Stuff It was set up with an apartment above the office to have someone live at the property, but it wasn't necessary since I lived in my grandparents' house next door. It also wasn't necessary for me to share that information with strangers.

"When are people here?" he asked.

His questions were starting to make me uncomfortable, but I answered anyway. "Our office hours are Monday through Saturday from ten to six. We're closed on Sundays."

He nodded and took a long look around the office. I was more than ready for him to leave when he finally spoke again. "Thanks for your time. I'll be back if I decide to go with you."

"Thanks for stopping by," I said and locked the door as soon as he was in his car.

"That was weird," I mumbled to myself and set about closing up shop for the day.

Once I got home, I couldn't stop thinking about the strange man and his questions. I wasn't sure if I was being paranoid or if there really was something odd about his visit, so I decided to call Landon and see what he thought.

But I couldn't find my phone. Anywhere.

After thoroughly searching the house, I picked up Kalen and went back to the office hoping I'd accidentally left it in my haste to get out of there. But it was nowhere to be found.

Sighing, I picked up the office phone and called Landon.

"Why are you calling me from Stuff It?" he asked immediately upon answering.

"Because I need your help."

"With what? I'm already in my PJs, so if it requires regular clothes, I'm out."

"I can't find my phone anywhere. I'm wondering if I may have accidentally thrown it away when I was taking out the trash," I said.

"What is it you need me to do?" he asked cautiously.

I wanted to laugh. He thought I was going to ask him to check the dumpster. "I need you to watch Kalen while I see if it's in one of the trash bags."

"Oh," he said sounding relieved. "Yeah, I can do that. You picking me up?"

"Of course. I'll be right there."

Since I didn't have to get on any roads, I strapped Kalen to my chest with the new baby carrier I'd picked up at the store and drove the golf cart over to get Landon.

"Where are you going?" he asked when I pulled up to the gate at Stuff It.

"To the dumpster to look for my phone."

"Oh," he said slowly. "You meant for me to watch him out here, not at your house."

"Um, yeah. I need you here in case something happens."

"Like what?" he asked as he glanced around nervously.

"Like me not being able to get out. I'd need you to help me."

"You better look before you leap, because I'm not carrying a baby into a dumpster to fish you out. That's a headline I'm not going to be."

"Do you want to hold him or wear this?" I asked and pointed to my chest.

"I'll wear the carrier," he said excitedly. "I've always wanted to try one of these. Oh, shhh! Don't tell anyone I said that."

"Okay, wish me luck," I said, after helping Landon get situated with Kalen.

"Good luck," he said and wrinkled his nose as I climbed into the dumpster. "Are you sure you've looked everywhere?"

I stuck my head through the side door and glared at him. "Do you honestly think I would be elbow deep in this disgusting dumpster if I hadn't looked everywhere?" I nearly shouted.

"Okay, honey. Calm yourself and finish your dumpster dive so we can get far away from this rancid smell."

"I hate to break it to you, but that rancid smell is coming from what's out there with you, not what's in here," I gleefully shared.

"No," Landon said in horror. "Say it ain't so."

"I'll say it, but it'll be a lie," I laughed.

"Look at you and your nephew giving me shit," Landon joked.

I picked up a bag of trash and started to look through it when an idea hit me. "Will you call my phone?"

"Yep. One sec," he said.

Moments later, Landon's designated ringtone filled the air. "It's here!" I said excitedly and held the trash bag up to see if I could spot the lighted screen. It stopped ringing before I found it, so Landon called again. Four phone calls later, I finally located it. "Got it!"

Landon's outstretched hand appeared through the door seconds later. "Give it to me and climb out. Hurry up, girlfriend. There's a bug that's been eyeballing me like a piece of meat. I don't like it."

"No, it's covered in…something. I'll put it in my pocket until we get back to the house."

"Do I need to spray you off with the hose before you go inside?" he teased.

"No," I giggled. "But I am going to take these clothes off in the garage."

"You don't have a garage," he pointed out.

"I have a covered carport. It's the same as a garage without doors."

"Yes! Without doors."

"Oh, please. Who's going to see me?"

"Anyone with a decent pair of binoculars," he said and gestured to the apartment buildings.

"Fine," I huffed. "Will you go inside and get me a towel to cover up with?"

"That I can do." When he returned, he held the towel up while I stripped down to my underwear. Then, he handed me a bathrobe. "Put that on. Wash your hands. Change the baby. Then, you can shower while I burn your clothes and anything else you touched."

I rolled my eyes at his dramatics. "It wasn't that bad."

"Yes, it was. You're in denial. Stop talking. Start washing."

I didn't need any encouragement. I felt like I was covered in filth and other unspeakable things. Once Kalen was clean, I handed him back to Landon and ran for my bathroom.

After I showered, I found Landon in the living room with Kalen sound asleep in his arms. "I was afraid I'd wake him if I moved," he whispered.

"I'll take him." He leaned forward and carefully placed Kalen in my arms.

When I returned to the living room, I joined Landon on the couch. "After you left today, this guy came into the store and kind of creeped me out."

"What happened?" he asked.

"He asked about renting a unit. I told him we didn't have any available and offered to add him to our waitlist. Then, he started asking questions about our security and when employees were on the premises. I don't know. The whole thing seemed weird, but maybe it wasn't. What do you think?"

"Did he seem like the type of person who would want to know those kinds of details to make an informed decision or was he more along the lines of someone who was casing the joint?" he asked.

"He definitely gave off casing vibes," I shuddered. "I hope he doesn't come back."

"He does look kind of creepy," Landon said while he stared at his phone.

I leaned over and looked at the security footage on his screen. "So, it wasn't just me?"

"Definitely not. You want to have a sleepover?" he asked knowingly.

"Yes," I answered immediately causing him to laugh. "I wasn't going to ask, but since you offered, I'm not going to say no."

"You know you can always ask," he said seriously.

"I know, and I would have if I was really worried. He just unnerved me a little. And then I lost my phone."

"Well, there's no need to worry. You found your phone, creepy guy is gone, and I'm here. Now, what do you have to eat? I'm starving."

8

GAME

When I got home from work, I went straight to the bathroom to shower. It had been a long week and I was trying to decide between staying home and relaxing or spending the evening at the clubhouse. While I was showering, my phone dinged with a text. I waited until I was finished to check the message and smiled when I saw who it was from.

Blakely: Hey. Are you busy?

Grant: Just got home from work. Something wrong?

Blakely: Maybe. I keep getting notifications for movement on the cameras. But I don't see anything when I try to play the video.

I wasn't going to attempt to troubleshoot through text messages, so I called her.

"What do you mean you can't see anything?" I asked when she picked up.

"When I tap the notification, it takes me to the video clip, which is nothing but a black screen for the entire clip," she explained.

"How many times has that happened?"

"I don't know. More than five, less than twenty," she guessed.

"What does the live feed show?"

She was silent for a few seconds, I assumed while she navigated to that screen. "A black screen."

I had no idea what the problem could be, and since I didn't have admin access like Judge did, there wasn't much I could do to help her remotely. Sure, I could have told her to call the support line, but I didn't want to pass up an opportunity to see her.

"Do you want me to come over and see what's going on?" I offered.

"Oh, no," she started. "I couldn't—"

"I won't tell if you won't," I said, repeating the words she said to me the day I met her.

She laughed lightly. "It's up to you. I'm not going to say no, but please don't go out of your way or make a special trip."

"Make sure you lock the doors and set your alarm. I'm leaving now."

"I will. Thanks, Grant."

"No problem. I'll be there soon," I said, already on my way out the door.

I didn't realize she'd already started babysitting until she opened the door with a crying infant in her arms.

I cringed and glanced at my bike. "Did I wake him?"

"No, he woke up crying right after we got off the phone, but I haven't figured out what's wrong yet. He's not hungry, and I just changed his diaper."

"I'm pretty good with babies. Want me to try?" I asked and held out my hands.

She didn't hesitate. "Yes, please."

I took the little guy into my arms and cradled him against my chest underneath my cut. Then, right beside his ear, I made a clicking sound by flicking the nail on my index finger with my thumbnail. Kalen stopped crying within the first minute and his eyes started to droop within the second.

"I don't know what you're doing, but keep doing it," she whispered.

"Where's his bed?" I whispered back.

"Follow me."

I continued clicking my nails next to his ear while she showed me to his room. Then, I carefully placed him in his bed and tiptoed out with Blakely right behind me.

"How did you do that?" she asked excitedly.

"I can't tell you; it's a secret," I smirked.

"I'll give you the lemonade recipe."

I laughed. "Oh, now you want to trade?"

"Yes. Your magic baby trick for my lemonade recipe," she stated and held out her hand for me to shake.

I placed my hand in hers. "Deal. But let's see what's happening with the cameras first."

With the notifications page on the screen, she passed

her phone to me. "Tap any of the ones on the first page."

"What the hell?" I mumbled after watching a few video clips.

"So, it's not just me?"

"No, not at all," I said and continued to study the screen. "Usually, when there's a black screen it means the cameras are offline, but yours are definitely online because they're still showing the current date and time. I'm gonna go over to the property and check the physical equipment. Do I need a code for the gate?"

"No, not anymore," she smiled and extended her hand for her phone. "I can buzz you in from here."

"I'll be right back," I told her and headed for the door.

She held up a set of keys. "Take the golf cart."

"Thanks."

I rolled to a stop and got out to inspect the camera at the front gate. As soon as my flashlight illuminated the device, I knew what the problem was—someone spray-painted the lens. I assumed the same would be true for the rest of the cameras, but I checked each one to be sure.

Oddly enough, only two of the cameras had been tampered with.

After checking the last of the devices, I turned the corner to go back to the house when a flash of light caught my attention.

Slowing to a stop, I got out and stood against the wall of the building while I waited to see or hear more.

Leaves rustled, followed by the sound of a twig

snapping. Then, the unmistakable sound of someone running.

I did a quick sweep of the area with my flashlight. "Hey!" I shouted when I spotted someone on the other side of the fence at the rear corner of the property.

When they took off running, so did I.

"Stop, motherfucker!" I yelled.

I was going to kick their ass twice when I caught them. Once for fucking with Blakely, and once for making me chase their punk ass.

"Grant!" Blakely shouted in the distance.

"Go back inside!" I yelled back and focused on clearing the fence in front of me.

"Please, Grant, come back!" The fear in her voice had me changing course without a second thought.

"Go inside and lock the door! I'm coming back!"

I jogged back to the golf cart and stomped on the gas pedal. When it didn't budge, I double tapped the pedal and pressed it to the floor again.

"Shiiiittt!" I shouted when the wheels spun seconds before the golf cart shot forward like it was running on jet fuel.

The brakes were useless. There was nothing I could do but hold on to the steering wheel and try not to crash into anything.

"Fuck!" The closed gate came into view, but I couldn't stop. Squeezing my eyes shut, I braced for an impact that never came.

When I opened my eyes again, I was through the gate and headed straight for Blakely's house. I held on to the steering wheel with a white-knuckle grip, ready to steer away from the house when the blasted contraption finally began to slow and the brakes I'd been relentlessly pressing started to respond.

She opened the screen door when she saw me coming, because she didn't have the door closed and locked like she should have.

"Does it always do that?" I asked, pointing to the possessed golf cart.

"It's something Papa did. I'll tell you about it later," she rushed out. "What happened? I heard shouting. And I thought I saw you running."

"I saw someone on the other side of the fence near the last row of buildings. They took off running when I shined my flashlight on them. I yelled for them to stop and chased after them when they didn't," I explained.

"They got away?"

I cupped her cheek. "I heard you yell, so I stopped chasing them and came back."

She tilted her head down and looked away from me. "I didn't know what was happening, and I didn't want you to get hurt."

"Too fucking sweet," I said and kissed the top of her head.

"Did you get a good look at the person?" she asked.

"I wouldn't call it a good look, but I would say they were in their late teens or early twenties, average height, thin build, fair skin. They were wearing a hat so I'm not sure about hair color."

"I hope you scared the crap out of them. Did you get a chance to look at the cameras?" she asked.

"Yes. Someone spray-painted over the lenses."

"Are you kidding me? Why would someone do that?" she asked incredulously.

"It's easier than taking them out and you're less likely to get caught if you approach the camera from behind and spray it from directly underneath," I explained.

"So, there's nothing wrong with the cameras?" she asked.

"I can't say for sure, but if it was just paint and nothing else, they'll be fine once they're cleaned off. But you should probably call the police first."

"Oh," she said, sounding surprised. "Do you think the person you saw is the one who spray-painted the cameras?"

"It'd be one hell of a coincidence if it wasn't them," I pointed out.

"Right. I need to check the units and make sure none of them were tampered with or broken into first."

"You sure?"

"Yeah. If nothing was stolen, then I don't see a need to involve the police. It was probably just some kid with nothing else to do."

I didn't agree with her, but it wasn't my call to make. Instead, I offered to check the property for her, so she didn't have to disturb the baby. And I wanted to see if the mystery person left anything behind.

After I rode through the property and checked every single unit, I stopped at each camera and cleaned the spray paint off the lenses. Then, I circled around to the rear corner and stopped to look around with my flashlight. Unfortunately, I didn't find anything helpful.

9

BLAKELY

When Grant left to check the units, I went to the kitchen intending to wash Kalen's bottles and wipe down the counters. Before I realized what I was doing, I was halfway through making banana pudding. I liked to bake when I was stressed, and I was definitely stressed.

When he started describing the person he chased, I couldn't help but think they sounded a lot like Ben even though I knew it couldn't be him because he was in jail. However, it didn't escape me that strange things had been happening around Stuff It since Ben's visit.

Part of me felt like I should mention my observations to Grant, but I didn't want to betray Ben's trust. On the other hand, I didn't really know Ben while Grant had proven himself to be trustworthy. I wasn't sure what to do.

Grant lightly knocked on the side door, causing me to jump.

"What are you doing?" he asked when I let him in.

"Huh? Oh, making something," I answered distractedly. "Was everything okay with the units?"

"I didn't see anything out of place, and every unit had a locked lock. I also cleaned off the lenses for you."

"Thank you," I said sincerely. "You didn't have to do that."

"I know. But I wanted to. When you get a chance to check the app, let me know if they're clear. It was hard to tell with a flashlight."

I washed my hands and put the covered dish in the refrigerator. "Would you like a cup of coffee or something else to drink?" I offered while I checked the camera feed.

"Does that mean you're out of lemonade?"

"It does," I laughed. "But the recipe's all yours as soon as you tell me what kind of baby magic you know."

He held up his thumb and index finger. "Flick your fingernails against each other next to his ear. I don't know what it is about that sound. It's almost like it lulls them into a trance. It's worked every time I've tried it."

I cleared my throat. "The secret lemonade recipe is a packet of Kool-aid. I use three-fourths of a cup of sugar instead of one cup and toss in a few lemon slices."

His mouth dropped open in shock. "Are you serious?"

"Cross my heart."

He pointed a finger at me. "I'm going to try this, so I'll know if you're giving me a bullshit recipe in an attempt to keep your secret."

"I pinky promise," I said and extended my little finger.

Without hesitation, he hooked his pinky with mine and we shook once. I grinned from ear-to-ear the whole time.

"So, yes or no on coffee?"

"That depends. Are we having anything else with coffee?" he asked and nodded to the refrigerator.

"That needs to chill for an hour or two before it can be served."

"Well," he clapped his hands together. "What do you want to do for the next hour or two?"

"We could watch a movie," I suggested.

"Sounds good to me. Do you have something in mind?"

"Actually, I do, but feel free to say no." At his nod, I continued. "There's a new shark movie I've been wanting to see. I love shark movies, but Landon won't watch them with me."

Grant laughed and made himself comfortable on my couch. "That's more than okay with me. I was bracing for a chick flick."

* * *

I WAITED QUIETLY AND WATCHED INTENTLY AS HE brought the spoon to his mouth and tasted the banana pudding. His reaction didn't take long. He closed his eyes and groaned, while sliding the spoon from his mouth. Then, he used it to point from me to his bowl and back. "This is great. Is it another one of your Nana's recipes?"

"Thank you," I beamed. "And yes, it is. Almost everything I make is one of hers."

I started cleaning the kitchen, hoping to get that done while he was eating, but he only took a few more bites before he wiped his mouth and asked, "Aren't you going to have any?"

"Oh, yeah, I'll get some in a minute," I said and went back to wiping off the counters.

I didn't hear him move, but I froze when I felt his presence behind me. Then, his bowl appeared on the counter beside my hand. He gently took the cloth I was using to clean and tossed it to the side. Turning me by my shoulders to face him, he hoisted me onto the countertop and met my eyes. "Have some now."

"Okay," I agreed quietly. He scooped some onto his spoon and turned back to me. I licked my lips and parted my mouth, ready for a bite of yummy goodness.

The spoon hit the counter with a loud clatter as Grant's lips crashed into mine, kissing me with an intensity that was almost too much. Which was exactly what I liked.

Eagerly returning the kiss, I wrapped my arms around his shoulders and tried to pull him closer while my legs went around his waist. My hands found their way to the hem of his shirt and started pushing it up. He reached behind his head for the collar of his shirt and yanked it off in one fluid motion.

He kissed his way from my lips to my ear. "I was trying to be good."

"I know. Stop it," I whined and punctuated it by

pinching his side. "I don't want you to be good. I want you to fuck me."

"Fuck," he growled, and then I was moving. In a matter of moments, I was naked from the waist down on my back on the kitchen island and Grant's face was between my legs.

"Oh!" I groaned when his mouth first touched me. "Do that again. Please. Please, please, please," I begged.

"This?" he asked and repeated the movement.

"Yes! That!" My shouts faded into a low moan when he slipped his fingers inside me. "Oh, fuck. I'm going to come."

I held my breath and waited for him to change his rhythm. It seemed like those words—I'm going to come—were the cue for a man to change what he was doing and therefore ruin the orgasm. But not Grant. He didn't falter, and I started to panic, because he was going to make me come in record time.

"No, no, wait," I breathed and pushed on his head.

His head shot up. His eyes full of concern. "I want to come on your cock," I panted.

"Baby, you're gonna be coming on my cock, my face, my fingers," he trailed off and started kissing my stomach. Then, he lifted me into his arms. "Where's your room?"

I pointed down the hall. "The one at the end."

His fingers dug into my ass when I started sucking on his ear as he carried me to my room. "You got a condom?" I whispered.

"Yeah, in my wallet."

"Hurry."

I landed on my bed with a bounce. "Get that shirt off," he barked.

I tossed my shirt to the side and smiled when I heard his jeans hit the floor. When I looked up, I saw a man on a mission, rolling a condom down his shaft and heading straight for me.

I spread my legs wider, in case he had any other thoughts about what we were doing. He climbed on the bed, positioned himself at my entrance, and pushed inside in one fluid movement, coming to a stop when his lips were over mine. "Fuck, you feel good."

"Please, move, Grant. Please," I whispered next to his ear. I wanted him so bad, and I didn't care how desperate I sounded.

When he moved, he ignited every nerve ending his body touched. I felt every part of him. Deeper than I ever imagined.

10

BLAKELY

Grant offered to pick us up to take us to the clubhouse for the party, but I'd had a hard time installing Kalen's car seat base in my car and didn't want to mess with transferring it to Grant's truck. Plus, the amount of stuff I needed to bring for Kalen was borderline embarrassing. I had never taken a baby anywhere overnight before, so I had no idea if I had packed an abnormal amount of stuff. But, I'd rather have something and not need it versus need something and not have it.

I sent Grant a text to let him know when we were on our way and followed the GPS directions to the Blackwings clubhouse. When I pulled into the parking lot, I saw Grant standing outside the front doors and smiled. He was waiting for us to arrive. He met me at my door and offered to carry Kalen inside while I got the diaper bag and the two containers of brownies I made. "We might have to make two trips," I said sheepishly. "I wasn't sure what he would need."

He chuckled. "Not a problem. Like I said before, there's quite a few club kids around here. Sometimes this place seems more like a toy factory than an MC clubhouse. What are those?" he asked and pointed to the containers.

"I know you said I didn't need to bring anything, but I made brownies."

"Of course you did," he smiled and stopped at the front doors before entering. "I hope you're ready to meet everyone."

I laughed nervously. "I'm as ready as I'll ever be."

As soon as we stepped inside, I was bombarded with introductions. I shook hands with and hugged more people than I could count.

"I'll never remember their names," I whispered to Grant.

He laughed. "No one expects you to. Come on, I'll show you where my room is as well as the kids' room."

I followed him through the crowded room to a long hallway lined with doors. "These are the members' bedrooms, and this one's mine."

He opened the door to a room that resembled a nice hotel room with a queen-size bed, a dresser, a recliner, and a large television. And it was exceptionally clean.

Grant noticed the surprised look on my face and chuckled. "I told you it wouldn't be what you expected."

"I like it," I said, instead of admitting that he was right.

"The kids' room is a few doors down, but if you'd rather keep Kalen in here, Layla has a portable crib you can use."

"Since he's so young, and this is a new environment for him, I think it'd be better for him to stay in here with me," I said and hoped I didn't sound rude.

Grant nodded. "I'll have the prospect bring the crib and set it up. What time does he usually go down for the night?"

"Usually around eight."

Grant looked at his watch. "That gives us about an hour. Do you want to go out to the common room until you need to get him ready for bed?"

"Sure," I said and lifted Kalen from his seat.

Once again, I was bombarded with people as soon as we entered the common room, but thankfully, their attention was focused on Kalen and not me.

"I'll be happy to hold him if you want to get something to eat," an older lady offered. "I'm Leigh, Judge's mom."

"She's everybody's mom," Grant added.

"Thank you. That'd be great. It's getting close to his bedtime, so he might get fussy soon."

"I'll bring him right to you if he does," she promised.

Grant led me to a table loaded with food—hamburgers, hot dogs, hot wings, and french fries.

I decided on a hamburger, fries, and hot wings, but Grant stopped me when I went to add the wings to my plate. "The ones on the left were made with regular hot sauce. The ones on the right are coated in the sauce Judge makes using Carolina Reapers."

"No thank you," I said and went for the wings on the left. "I like to be able to taste my food when I eat it."

Grant laughed. "Me too. His wings are way too hot for me."

"I should've known something was different since there's still so many on the plate."

"At the end of the night, most of the food will be gone, but there'll still be plenty of his hot wings left."

"You talking shit about my food?" Judge asked from behind Grant.

"Stating the facts, brother," Grant shot back.

Judge shrugged. "They're not for everyone."

"Did you make the other wings too?" I asked.

He shook his head. "I used to, but I was relieved of my duties after an unfortunate incident where I cross-contaminated the sauces."

"Oh, no," I gasped.

"Oh, yes," Grant laughed. "It was a regular night at the clubhouse when all of a sudden chaos erupted. Then, we ran out of milk. It was bad."

"I've always wondered what the super-hot peppers were like, but I've been too scared to try one," I shared.

"I haven't had one either. I was one of the lucky ones the night of the great mix-up," Grant said and walked to a table where we joined another couple. "This is Coal and his Old Lady Aspen," Grant introduced.

"Nice to meet you. I'm Blakely," I said and took a seat.

"Nice to meet you too," Aspen said. "So, how did you two meet?"

"We met when I was helping Judge get caught up on service calls. I went out to repair the security cameras and upgrade the system at her business," Grant answered.

"What kind of business?" Coal asked.

"It's a storage unit facility called Stuff It," I said.

Aspen laughed. "That's a great name!"

"Thanks," I smiled. "My Nana came up with it."

"That's the place beside The Brooklands, right?" Coal asked.

I nodded and wiped my lips with a napkin while I hurried to swallow the food in my mouth. "Yes, it is. My grandparents sold the land to the apartment developers and then opened a storage facility on the land they kept."

"That's genius," Aspen said.

"It's worked out well for our family."

A large man with a friendly smile walked up to our table. "Sorry to interrupt, but I overheard your story about your grandparents. Are you Conway Collins's granddaughter?"

"Yes, I am," I smiled. "Do you know him?"

He grinned. "I haven't talked to him in years, but he was once a good buddy of mine. I've met you once before, but you were probably too young to remember me."

I took a good look at his face, and suddenly, I knew exactly who he was. "You gave me a sucker after you helped Nana with her dead battery."

"That'd be me," he grinned. "My name's Bear."

"I just told Grant that story the other day."

Grant nudged me with his elbow. "Tell him the rest of it."

I laughed and covered my face with my hand. "This is so embarrassing. I was little, okay? I didn't know the right words, so when we got home and Papa asked where I got the sucker, I told him a big man in leather gave it to me after Nana jacked him off."

Bear threw his head back and laughed, as did the rest of the table. "I can't believe Conway never told me about that. How's your grandpa doing?"

"He's good. He had a bout with non-Hodgkin's lymphoma a few years ago, but he's been in remission since he completed treatment. Him and Nana bought an RV and are traveling around the country."

"Tell him I said hello the next time you talk to him. And I'd love to see him when they're in town sometime," he said.

"I'll tell him. They usually make a trip home once during the summer, and they're always back for the holidays."

Bear looked up at the sound of his name being called from across the room and then he chuckled. "It looks like my pregnant wife is still hungry. I'll catch up with y'all later."

I looked across the room and saw two pregnant women sitting at a table together. "Which one is his wife?" I asked curiously.

"The one laughing. The other one is his son's wife," Aspen said.

"They're pregnant at the same time?" I blurted and immediately covered my mouth with my hand. "Sorry! I didn't mean that the way it sounded."

Aspen laughed. "It's fine. I mean, it is a unique situation."

Thankfully, Grant jumped in and changed the subject, saving me from the awkward moment. "You two have something in common. I think Aspen enjoys cooking as much as you do."

"I'm not the only one talented in the kitchen," she grinned. "Game puts me to shame when it comes to decorating cupcakes."

"Really?" I asked in surprise. "How did that happen?"

"It's a secret," he said cryptically.

"He won't tell me, but maybe you can get it out of him," Aspen teased.

I turned my head at the sound of a baby crying and saw Leigh making her way over to us. "I think someone's ready for bed," she said and handed a grumpy Kalen to me.

"He lasted longer than I thought he would," I told her. "Thanks for watching him."

"You're welcome. I just love babies," she beamed.

"We'll be back in a little bit," Grant told Coal and Aspen. "Save us some seats."

"Will do," Coal said and wrapped his arm around Aspen's shoulders.

I made quick work of changing Kalen's diaper and dressing him in his pajamas. Then, I opened a bottle of water and poured the designated amount into his bottle before adding the formula. I shook it and started feeding him.

"Um, aren't you supposed to warm that?" Grant asked carefully.

"He won't drink it warm," I shrugged. "He'll spit it out and push it away until it's cool, then he'll drink it. Once I figured that out, I started doing it this way."

Kalen's eyes started to droop halfway through his bottle, and he was sound asleep by the time he finished. I carefully placed him in the portable crib and exhaled in relief when he didn't stir. Occasionally, I would think he was asleep and put him down only for his eyes to pop open two seconds before he started crying.

I picked up the baby monitor and gave Grant a thumbs up. We quietly left the room and closed the door behind us.

When we returned to the common room, the tables and chairs had been rearranged in a semi-circle around a large screen hanging from the ceiling. Coal and Aspen were seated at a table front and center with two seats saved for us.

"How'd you guys end up with the best seats in the house?" I asked.

Grant grinned. "Coal's brother is fighting in the main event. He always gets the good seats, which is why I asked him to save two for us. Perks of being his best friend."

I'd never watched an organized fight before. The first couple of matches were okay to watch, but it was hard for me to get into it without having a designated person to cheer for. I didn't know anything about the fighters, so it didn't matter to me who won. Grant and

Coal seemed to be having a great time, and I enjoyed chatting with Aspen between rounds.

But as the night went on, I struggled to stay awake, and I eventually fell asleep on Grant's shoulder. I woke when the entire room erupted in cheers and looked at the screen to see a man who strongly resembled Coal with his arms raised in the air.

"Did he win?" I asked through a yawn.

"Yeah, he did," Grant said proudly. "You ready for bed?"

I nodded and yawned again. "Yeah. Sorry for falling asleep. I'm never up this late."

"I liked having you snuggled up against me all night."

Yeah, I liked that part too, and I was looking forward to snuggling up against him for the rest of the night.

11

GAME

I hadn't seen Blakely since the morning after she spent the night at the clubhouse, and I couldn't wait any longer. I didn't care if I looked overeager. I liked her, and despite my road name, I wasn't interested in playing games.

So, I decided to order takeout and surprise her with dinner. As I walked to her door, I glanced at the bag of food I was carrying and wondered if I'd made the right decision.

Before I could continue second guessing myself, she pushed the door open and smiled. "What are you doing here?"

I held up the bag of food. "I brought dinner. Are you hungry?"

"Yes," she answered immediately. "You have perfect timing. I was just about to heat up some leftovers."

I followed her inside and placed the food on the kitchen counter. The house was filled with the smell of cinnamon, brown sugar, and apples. If she had a homemade apple pie in the oven, I was going to have to marry her. "What smells so good?"

"Apple pie," she confirmed and I almost groaned. "Landon's been asking me to make one. It's his favorite."

"Does Landon share?"

She laughed. "He's not getting the whole pie. Just a few slices. It's almost done, so you can have some after we eat."

As soon as the words left her mouth, the timer on the oven beeped. She turned it off and donned her oven mitts just as the sound of a baby crying filled the air.

"Want me to get him?" I asked.

"Yes, please. He's in the living room," she said and removed the pie from the oven. "Be careful! We've been having an issue with leaky diapers recently."

"Thanks for the heads up," I said flatly and returned to the kitchen carrying a pee-soaked baby with my arms fully extended.

She tossed the oven mitts to the side and reached for Kalen. "Sorry about that. I'll get him cleaned up and be right back."

While she was gone, I washed my hands in the kitchen sink so I could start divvying out our dinner.

"I didn't realize you'd be babysitting again," I said when she returned. "I probably should've called instead of dropping by unannounced."

"I guess I didn't tell you. Kalen's staying with me for a few weeks while his mother is out of town for work," she explained.

"A few weeks?" I asked in surprise.

"Yeah. She was in a pinch, and I was able to help out," she said and abruptly changed the subject. "So, how did you learn how to decorate cupcakes?"

"YouTube," I said honestly.

"Okay, but why?"

I sighed. "I don't mind telling you, but it's not exactly a great story."

Her eyes softened. "I'm enjoying getting to know you, so I'd still like to hear it. I want to know all of your stories, not just the good ones."

I think that was the moment I realized she was perfect. Or at least perfect for me.

"I have a niece, Dani, who's a few years younger than me. She moved in with us when my sister was sent to prison. My mother went overboard and planned this elaborate party for the first birthday she spent with us. While my mother was getting things set up for the party, she sent me and Dani to pick up the custom cupcakes she ordered. Dani sat in the back on the way home to make sure the cupcakes didn't slide off the seat. I honestly don't know if she wasn't paying attention or if she did it herself, but when we got home, the cupcakes were in the floor and completely ruined. Dani proceeded to tell my mother that it happened because I was driving recklessly. My mother told me to figure out how to replace the cupcakes before the party or I would be grounded for a month. So, I found some videos to watch and redecorated store-bought cupcakes. They would never admit it, but I think my cupcakes turned out better than the original ones."

"Grant," Blakely said sympathetically. "Were they always like that?"

"Pretty much," I nodded. "It wasn't as bad before my dad died, and it got much worse after my sister was arrested."

"How are things now?"

"Fine for me. I got out of there as soon as I turned eighteen. I didn't even try to maintain a relationship with them because it was always one-sided. I completely cut ties with them," I explained.

"That must've been hard for you."

"It actually wasn't. I joined the MC not long after I made the decision and found a family with them. For a long time, I hoped things would change with my biological family. I had to let go of that hope to heal. And it's a good thing I did because nothing's changed. My mother called me a few weeks ago because she hadn't been able to get in touch with Dani. She insisted that I help her and sent the cops to the gym to question me when I refused."

Blakely's eyes widened in surprise. "What did you tell them?"

"I told them the truth. That I wasn't in contact with my mother or niece and didn't have any information to give them. Well, I did mention that Dani was known to disappear when she didn't get her way."

"Is she still missing?"

I shrugged. "I have no idea. I haven't heard anything else from my mother or the police."

"No wonder you didn't want to tell Aspen about the

cupcakes," she said as Kalen started to fuss. "Sorry, I need to get him ready for bed."

"I should probably get going," I said and got to my feet while she went to get Kalen.

"You don't have to leave," she said. "He'll be asleep in about thirty minutes, and then I'll be free for the rest of the evening."

Blakely had just returned to the living room when the side door opened, and someone stepped inside. Instinctively, I stood up and pushed her behind me, ready to defend her from the intruder.

The man held his hands up in surrender. "I'm just here for the pie."

Blakely gently squeezed my arm and stepped out from behind me. "Grant, this is my best friend, Landon. Landon, this is Grant."

Landon looked at me then back to Blakely with his hands still in the air. "Is he going to break me if I move?"

I chuckled and stepped forward with my hand extended to shake his. "Sorry, man. I wasn't expecting anyone to come in and just reacted. It's nice to meet you. I've heard a lot about you."

Landon smiled and shook my hand. "It's nice to meet you too."

"Do you want to stay for pie, or do you want to take yours home?" Blakely asked.

"I'll stay. Unless I'm interrupting something," he said and raised his eyebrows.

"You're not interrupting anything," Blakely said dismissively. "I just put Kalen down for the night."

"Great! Let's eat," Landon said and made himself at home in the kitchen.

"How long have you two known each other?" I asked.

"Almost ten years," Blakely said. "We met on the first day of high school."

Landon laughed. "You should've asked how we met."

"Okay, how did you meet?"

"We met when she tried to kill me."

Blakely groaned. "That's not what happened."

"Hush. I'm telling it," Landon said. "The school randomly assigned lockers. Blakely's locker was above mine. We both went to our lockers after first period. She dropped her English literature textbook on my head and almost knocked me out. After she made sure I was okay, she offered to share her top locker with me, and we've been besties ever since."

They continued sharing stories from high school while Landon devoured two slices of pie.

"You two enjoy the rest of your evening. Thanks for the pie, B," Landon said and showed himself out.

The moment he left, I hooked my finger in Blakely's belt loop and pulled her to me, kissing her as soon as her chest made contact with mine. I'd been itching to get my hands on her and couldn't wait any longer.

She returned the kiss with fervor and threaded her fingers through my hair.

Things escalated quickly. Within minutes she had her legs wrapped around my waist and I was carrying her to her bedroom.

12

BLAKELY

"What's going on with the weather?" Landon asked when he came back inside from checking locks. "It's crazy windy outside."

"There's a line of strong thunderstorms headed our way and another one right behind it," I said. "The first round is supposed to begin around ten o'clock tonight. They're expecting heavy rain, frequent lightning, strong winds, hail, and possibly tornadoes." I was always on top of the weather forecasts because I was terrified of lightning. I never wanted to be caught out and about in the middle of a storm, so I did my best to make sure I always knew when one was expected. And if I happened to be out somewhere when one popped up, I stayed put until it was over.

"Sounds like we should have a movie night at your place," Landon suggested. "Want to watch *Twister*?"

I laughed. "I was just about to ask if you wanted to spend the night." Landon's apartment was on the top floor of a three-story building. I always invited him over when tornadoes were expected. "And you already know the answer to that." Despite my hatred of real-life storms, *Twister* was one of my favorite movies. Landon and I watched it at least five times during each tornado season.

Landon took me and Kalen home after we closed Stuff It for the day and took the golf cart to his place to pack a bag before coming back to my house.

"What are we having for dinner?" he asked as soon as he stepped inside. "I'm starving."

"You're always starving," I pointed out.

"I can't help it. I have a fast metabolism. Now, feed me before I waste away into nothing," he teased.

"I was thinking about ordering something for delivery. Is that an asshole thing to do when it's storming?"

"It might be if you ordered during the height of the storm, but it's not even raining yet. Where are we ordering from?"

Before I could toss out some suggestions for us to debate, my phone rang. I smiled when I saw Grant's name on the screen. "Hello?"

"Hey. You busy?"

"No. Landon and I are trying to decide what to order for dinner. Would you like to join us?"

"Well, I was calling to see if you wanted to come with me to the clubhouse for the night. We're supposed to have some bad storms tonight with possible tornadoes. The clubhouse has a basement, and we also have generators if we lose power. Landon is welcome to come too," he said.

I moved the phone away from my mouth to ask Landon, but he was already nodding his head yes. "Yes, we'll come with you."

"Great. I'm leaving my house now. I'll be there in about fifteen minutes to pick you guys up."

I ended the call and hurried to my room to pack a bag. Then, I rushed around the house gathering everything Kalen would need.

"We're still going to get food, right?" Landon asked while he entertained Kalen.

I laughed. Sometimes, he had a one-track mind. "Yes. We can either stop and pick up something on the way to the clubhouse or order something when we get there."

When Grant arrived, we transferred the car seat base to his truck and loaded our bags. I opted to ride in the back seat with Kalen. The storms hadn't started yet, but judging by the dark clouds rolling in, it wouldn't be long before they did. And the less I could see, the better.

"Does he know about you and storms?" Landon asked once we were on our way.

"Not yet. An opportunity hadn't presented itself until now," I said and directed my next words to Grant. "I don't like storms. At all. I'm usually okay as long as I'm inside, and I prefer to be as far away from windows as possible."

"Then the clubhouse will be the perfect place for you. My room doesn't have any windows and neither does the basement," he said.

I was surprised by his response. Except for my grandparents, Landon was the only person who didn't make a big deal about it, until Grant. Usually, when I shared my fear of storms with people, they either wanted to know why or they would tell me the chances of being struck by lightning were slim to none. To be honest, I didn't understand why more people weren't bothered by storms. For me, it felt like Mother Nature was forcing me to play Russian roulette with bolts of electricity.

Landon clapped his hands together and changed the subject. "Let's talk about food. What are we doing for dinner?"

"Copper's having pizzas delivered," Grant said.

"See, Blakely, you're not the only asshole in town," Landon joked.

"You said I wasn't being an asshole!"

"What are y'all talking about?" Grant asked.

"Before you called, we were going to have something delivered. I asked Landon if ordering food for delivery during a storm was an asshole thing to do and he said no," I explained.

Grant smiled. "You really are the most considerate person I've ever met."

"Thank you," I beamed. "I try to treat others how I'd want to be treated."

Lightning flashed and caused me to flinch. I quickly closed my eyes and ducked my head while I waited for the impending rumble of thunder. A notification dinged on my phone. I knew it was the weather app telling me a lightning strike was within ten miles of my location, but I didn't want to open my eyes to check and see how close it actually was. Thankfully, Landon didn't have the same problem. "It's okay, B. It was eight miles away."

"How far are we from the clubhouse?" I asked.

"About two minutes," Grant answered. "The parking lot will likely be packed, so I'll pull up to the front doors and let you guys out."

"Thank you," I said with a tremendous amount of relief.

When we arrived at the clubhouse, Grant asked Layla to show us to his room while he parked the truck. I was glad he did, because I didn't want to awkwardly stand in the common room waiting for him. I was still in that weird zone where I wasn't uncomfortable around the club members, but I wasn't comfortable enough to move around by myself. Plus, I wasn't sure I remembered which door belonged to him.

"I hope you guys are hungry. Copper ordered a ton of pizza, which should be here any minute," Layla said.

"I am," Landon announced shamelessly.

"Come on out to the common room once you get settled and make yourselves comfortable wherever you can find a spot. We're expecting a full house tonight," she said.

"Thank you. We really appreciate you inviting us to spend the night," I told her.

"I'm glad you could join us. And I'm sure Game is too," she smiled and opened the door to his room. "I'll see you in a few minutes."

Landon dropped into a chair and took in Grant's room. "This is not what I was expecting."

"I know, right? I thought the same thing," I admitted.

He reached down beside the chair and felt around for a lever. "Is this a recliner? Oh, hell yes," he said as his feet were lifted into the air. "This is where I'm sleeping tonight."

Grant walked in while Landon was making his declaration and laughed. "That chair sleeps great. It might even be more comfortable than the bed."

Landon smirked and pointed an accusatory finger at me. "It will be for me. She kicks."

I gasped in mock indignation. "I do not."

"The bruise you left on my thigh the last time I spent the night says otherwise."

"Aren't you hungry? We should feed you before you get hangry," I said.

"The pizzas just arrived," Grant announced, effectively ending our bickering.

"Say no more," Landon said and made a beeline for the common room.

I didn't know what it was, but something happened with Landon between leaving Grant's room and eating dinner in the common room. He was quiet, and he was never quiet.

I waited until we finished eating and were back in Grant's room before I asked Landon what was going on. I didn't care if we were in the middle of a terrible storm, if one of the bikers made him uncomfortable, we were going home.

"Okay, so I told you about the guy I met recently. The one I've been on a few dates with?" Landon started.

"Yeah," I nodded. "What about him?"

"B, you can't say anything."

"I won't," I promised.

Landon looked around like he was checking to make sure we were alone. "He's here."

"What?" I shouted and slapped my hand over my mouth. Then, I lowered my voice. "He's a biker?"

"I think so," Landon said. "He was wearing a leather vest. He wouldn't be wearing one if he wasn't a member, would he?"

"I don't think so, but I don't really know. Which one is he?"

Landon pulled out his phone and showed me a picture. "This is Lance."

"That's Spazz," I told him. "And yes, he's a patched member. I met him last weekend."

Landon started to pace the room. "This isn't good. I shouldn't be here."

"Why the hell not?" I demanded.

"What if they don't like people like me?" he asked quietly.

"Then we'll leave," I said simply. "If they don't like you, I don't like them."

Landon pulled me in for a hug. "Thanks, B."

"You don't have to thank me. You're my best friend. This is what I do," I said.

We both jumped when someone suddenly knocked on the door. Grant was still downstairs helping get the basement ready in case we needed to move down there when the storms hit, so I wasn't sure if I was supposed to answer the door.

"It's Spazz."

My eyes widened in surprise as did Landon's. "Answer the door," he mouthed.

"You answer it," I mouthed back.

Spazz knocked again. "I know you're in there."

Landon turned the knob and pushed me in front of the door as he stepped behind it. "Hey, Spazz. How's it going?" I asked awkwardly.

He grinned. "Hey, Blakely. I wanted to talk to Landon. Can I come in?"

"Sure," I said and stepped to the side so he could enter. Spazz closed the door behind him, and I had no idea what to do. I glanced between the two of them. "If you two need a minute, I can step into the bathroom."

"Does she know?" Spazz asked quietly.

"She does," Landon confirmed.

"You don't need to leave," Spazz said and turned back to Landon. "I wasn't expecting to see you here, and I didn't know how to react," he started and shook his head. "I mean, I didn't know how you wanted me to react. I wasn't sure how open you are, and I didn't want to make you uncomfortable."

Landon's forehead wrinkled in confusion. "Wait. Are you saying they don't have a problem with it?"

"Who's the one being judgmental now?" Spazz laughed. "They don't care. I wouldn't have wanted to be a member if they did."

"Oh, well, in that case, I have nothing to hide," Landon said.

Spazz smiled. "Great. You want to crash in my room tonight?"

"I'd like that," Landon said softly and turned to me. "You okay if I ditch you?"

"I'll be fine," I assured him.

Grant returned to find me reading in bed while Kalen slept in the portable crib Layla brought to the room earlier. "Where's Landon?" he asked.

"He's in Spazz's room."

"Do they know each other?" he asked carefully.

"Yeah. They've been on a few dates, but Landon didn't know Spazz was a member until tonight," I told him.

"Is that why he was acting weird at dinner?" Grant asked. I hadn't realized he noticed the change in Landon and was impressed that he did.

"Yep. Spazz stopped by your room, they talked, and all is well," I said.

"Are you ready for bed?" he asked.

"Yes and no. I'm tired, but I never sleep well when the weather's bad," I explained.

"You don't have to worry about it tonight. Splint, Spazz, and Drew are staying up to monitor the weather. They'll wake us up if we need to move to the basement," he said as someone lightly knocked on the door.

He opened it to reveal Landon and Spazz. "We're still on for movie night, right?" Landon asked.

I smiled and looked at Grant. "Landon and I were planning on watching *Twister* at my house before you invited us to the clubhouse. Can we watch it in here?"

Grant chuckled. "That's an interesting choice, but

yeah, I'm down for movie night. Do you want me to go get some snacks from the kitchen?"

Spazz held up the bag he was carrying. "Already taken care of."

Landon climbed onto the bed beside me and we scooted to the middle to make room for Grant and Spazz. It was a tight fit, but I had no complaints because I felt safe and secure squished between my new man and my best friend. It wasn't long before I was fast asleep.

* * *

I WOKE WITH A START TO LANDON GENTLY SHAKING MY shoulder. "Get up, B. We need to get downstairs," he said urgently. "I'll get Kalen. Wake up Grant and get the diaper bag."

"I'm awake," Grant said and got out of bed.

"Is there a tornado?" I asked as we hurried downstairs. There were several people already in the basement and many more coming down behind us.

Before Landon could answer, cell phones started going off with emergency notifications.

"There's a tornado on the ground about three miles from here, and it's headed in our general direction," Landon said quietly and led us to a corner of the main room. He gestured to the chairs lining the wall. "Will this spot work for you?"

"Anything below ground is perfect," I said honestly and took a seat. He handed Kalen to me. He hadn't fully woken up, and I was hoping he would go back to sleep once we were situated.

Grant placed Kalen's infant carrier on the floor in front of me. "I wasn't sure how long we'd be down here, so I brought this in case you want to put him down."

"That was a great idea," I said. "He does get heavy after a while, and he'll probably sleep better without being shifted around every few minutes."

I placed Kalen in his seat and gently rocked him until he appeared to be sound asleep again. Then, I sat back in my chair and waited.

Grant, Landon, and Spazz did their best to distract me, but their attempts were in vain. Even in the basement, the storm was loud. I could clearly hear the wind howling and thunder booming. Then, almost as if someone flipped a switch, everything stopped, and silence surrounded us.

I moved from my chair to the floor and scooted Kalen beside me. Grant did the same and placed himself on the other side of Kalen's seat. Landon filled the spot on the other side of me and took my hand in his. Giving it a gentle squeeze, he whispered, "It'll be over soon."

"I hope so," I whispered back.

The imaginary switch flipped again, bringing the wind and thunder back with a vengeance. Cracks and crashes could be heard in the distance, and I could only imagine what they were—likely trees snapping and houses being demolished.

I closed my eyes and tried to focus on the breathing exercises I learned to help with my anxiety. I counted with each inhale and exhale, over and over, until the noises outside started to fade.

"We're not in the clear yet, but the worst of it is over," Spazz announced to the room.

"Are you sure?" I asked.

He turned his laptop toward me so I could see the screen. "Yes," he said confidently. "We're this dot right here, and this is the cell that produced the tornado. The storm isn't completely over, but it's safe to go back upstairs as far as the weather is concerned."

"What does that mean?" I asked, trying not to overreact to his words.

"A few of the brothers will go up first to make sure there wasn't any structural damage to the clubhouse. Once they say it's clear, we can go back to our rooms," he explained.

I glanced at the time on my phone. It was almost four o'clock in the morning. I highly doubted that I would be able to go back to sleep once we were allowed to go upstairs.

13

BLAKELY

I wasn't the only one who couldn't sleep after the events of the night. The majority of the clubhouse stayed awake. Thankfully, Kalen didn't have the same problem.

Around five, a few of the Old Ladies started cooking breakfast, and I volunteered to help. I needed something to do other than worry about the status of my home and business. I was trying to wait until the sun was up before asking Grant to drive me home, but it felt like the time was passing at a snail's pace.

The rain stopped shortly after we finished eating and it was light outside. I couldn't wait any longer. "I need to go to Stuff It and see if the units have any damage," I told Grant. According to the news, several tornadoes touched down in our area, leaving widespread damage behind.

He must have picked up on the urgency in my voice because he didn't argue with me like I'd expected.

"Okay. I can take you over there now. Are you ready to go?"

"Let me find Landon and see if he will watch Kalen. Then, I'm ready."

"I'm right here," Landon said from behind me. "I'll take care of the little munchkin. Go make sure we still have a place to work."

I gasped at his words. The thought of total destruction hadn't occurred to me. I was hoping for the place to be untouched but realistically expecting there to be some minor damage to deal with.

Landon placed his hand on my shoulder. "I'm sure everything's fine. And if it isn't, we'll take care of it like we always do. Do you want me to go with you?"

"I can watch Kalen until you get back," Layla offered.

"That'd be great," I said, not bothering to hide my relief. "I'm not sure how long we'll be gone."

She waved her hand dismissively. "I'm not going anywhere anytime soon."

"Thank you. I'll be back as soon as I can," I promised.

After making sure Layla had everything she might need for Kalen, I squeezed into Grant's truck with Landon, Spazz, Coal, and Drew. Aspen wanted to come with us, but Coal didn't think it was a good idea, and judging by the look on Aspen's face, I had a feeling she'd be letting him know exactly what she thought about that when he got back.

It took us at least twice as long to get to Stuff It as it normally would, but it felt even longer to me. I was already anxious to get there, but my anxiety grew as Grant navigated around fallen trees and flooded roads.

Landon reached over and gently pried my clasped hands apart. "Your fingers need circulation to function properly," he said softly.

"Thank you," I whispered and rested my head on his shoulder.

"Close your eyes. I'll let you know when we get there."

I did as he said. Even though I knew things could be bad in one area and fine in another, seeing the damage along the way was only making things worse for me.

Finally, Landon squeezed my hand as the truck began to slow. "It's not bad. Maybe a little roof damage, but everything's still standing."

I opened my eyes and exhaled in relief as I quickly scanned over the buildings. "Oh, thank goodness. I really thought the place was going to be leveled," I admitted.

We got out and made quick work of surveying the buildings. We didn't find anything other than the roof damage Landon pointed out when we first arrived, and thankfully, it was minimal. Only three units were affected—one with a car and some boxes, one with a boat and water sports equipment, and the one containing Ben's belongings.

I went to the office to notify the customers and the insurance company while the guys covered the roof with tarps. To my surprise, both customers opted to keep their things in their current units, which left me with Ben's unit to contend with. Since his unit had the most damage and contained items that shouldn't be exposed to the elements, I thought it would be best to move everything. Unfortunately, I didn't have another unit available. The only space I had was the empty caretaker's apartment above the office. It would have to do, but I didn't know how to explain what I was doing. Grant and his friends wouldn't think anything of it, but Landon would know something was up. First of all, the customer should be the one moving their items, not us, and certainly not into what should be the personal living space of the groundskeeper.

I jolted when Landon's voice startled me from my thoughts. "The tarps are up. Were you able to get in touch with the customers?"

"Yes," I nodded and got to my feet. "Two of the units are fine as they are, but we need to move the contents of the unit on the end to the apartment upstairs until the roof is repaired."

Landon cocked his head to the side. "Isn't this the new guy? The one who didn't want to come to the office?"

"Yes, that's the one," I confirmed, surprised by his recollection.

"Blakely," he said slowly. "What in the hell's going on?"

"It's a long story, but I promise I'll explain later."

"Okay, but for the record, I don't like any of this."

"I don't either," I whispered quietly, making sure he didn't hear me.

With six people helping, it didn't take long to load the back of Grant's truck with Ben's boxes and move them to the apartment. A few of the boxes had gotten wet with rain, so I had the guys place them on the far side of the room instead of stacking them with the others so I could open them and let them dry out some. The first two boxes I opened were full of clothes. The third one had sheets and blankets. But it was the fourth box that had me slowly closing the flaps and using every bit of strength I had to contain the panic wanting to explode from me. Because it was full of guns. Guns that I instinctively knew were not legally acquired. I didn't want to open the fifth box, but I had to know. Especially since Grant had commented on how heavy it was. I slowly slid the box cutter through the tape and carefully lifted the flap only to slam it back down as soon as my eyes landed on the handle of a pistol. My heart started racing and my hands began to shake.

"Blakely," Grant barked. "Are you okay?" he asked, his voice full of concern as he approached me. "You look like you've seen a ghost."

"Uh, now that you mention it, I don't feel so great," I said shakily. "Maybe I need to eat something."

"Let me help you downstairs," he said and gripped my arm. "Do you have anything to eat in your office?"

"I think so," I said and used my free hand to wipe the sweat from my forehead.

Grant led me downstairs to my office, and Landon followed along behind us, veering off to the break room to grab a drink and a pack of fruit snacks. "I'll stay with her while you guys finish up," Landon offered.

Grant looked like he wanted to protest, so I chimed

in before he could. "Go ahead. I'll be fine," I assured him.

"We'll hurry so we can get you out of here," he promised and placed a kiss on my cheek.

As soon as he was gone, Landon turned to face me. "You might've fooled him, but not me. You just had breakfast. Start talking, B."

I inhaled deeply and momentarily considered playing dumb, but I obviously needed help, and the only way I was going to get it was by telling someone what was going on. At the very least, I needed someone else's opinion, because I had no idea what to do.

"Unit three-seventy-three is the unit Ben rented from me," I said quietly. "That's his stuff we're moving upstairs."

"Yeah, I figured as much. What's that got to do with this?" he asked and waved his hand toward me to indicate my state of panic.

I swallowed thickly. I knew I needed to tell him, but I wasn't sure if I was ready for the can of worms I'd inadvertently opened. "The last two boxes I opened to let dry out were full of guns."

Landon blinked but didn't say a word. I was about to ask if he heard me when he finally came back online. "Unless your brother is an avid collector of firearms, I think you need to tell Grant."

"What? No! I haven't known him that long. This isn't his problem to deal with," I argued.

"It doesn't matter. We both know the Blackwings are good people. I don't know what to do, and neither do you, but I bet they will," Landon countered.

"Shouldn't I talk to Ben first?"

"How? You can't go to the jail and ask him about the boxes of guns he left in your storage unit without getting both of you in trouble."

"I can't just hand over his stuff to the local motorcycle club."

"You can if it's your ass or his. I guarantee someone's looking for those. And you don't want to be the one found with them. Especially now that they're inside the office building instead of in a unit."

He was right, and I knew it, but I still continued to argue. "I don't see how anyone would even think to look here. The unit wasn't in his name. There's nothing connecting the two of us."

"Except your mother. It wouldn't be hard to figure out Ben has a sister who runs a storage facility owned by her grandparents," he pointed out.

"Fuck," I breathed and covered my face with my hands.

"I know you feel some sort of obligation to Ben, but he didn't give any consideration to your safety and well-being when he chose to leave you with the smoking guns, so to speak. You and Kalen could be in danger. You could've been this whole time, and no one had any idea."

I nodded in agreement as a seed of anger sprouted inside me. Ben had put me and his son in danger. At the very least, he should've given me some kind of warning. "You're right. About everything," I conceded. "I don't want to do it here, but I'll talk to Grant as soon as we get back to the clubhouse."

14

GAME

I hurried up the stairs with the last box from my truck. Something was wrong with Blakely, and I wanted to get back downstairs to check on her. I knew Landon would take care of her, but I still didn't like leaving her in the state she was in.

I was on my way back to Blakely's office to see if she was ready to go when I overheard Blakely and Landon talking. Their words stopped me in my tracks. "…he didn't give any consideration to your safety and well-being when he chose to leave you with the smoking guns, so to speak. You and Kalen could be in danger. You could've been this whole time, and no one had any idea."

"You're right. About everything," she said. "I don't want to do it here, but I'll talk to Grant as soon as we get back to the clubhouse."

I wanted to barge in and demand she tell me everything right then and there, but something stopped me. Instead, I took a deep breath and tried to pretend like I didn't overhear their conversation. "How are you feeling?" I asked.

She gave me a weak smile. "Much better."

"We're finished with the boxes. Are you ready to go?"

"Yes, I just need to lock up and set the alarm," she said and got to her feet.

We rode back to the clubhouse in an uncomfortable silence. Once again, Blakely had her hands clasped tightly together in her lap, but Landon didn't intervene like he had before. He was usually quick to ease her worries if he could. The fact that he wasn't trying to soothe her made me even more curious as to what was going on.

By the time we arrived at the clubhouse, I'd imagined all sorts of stories she'd tell me, and none of them were good. It was all I could do to keep from throwing her over my shoulder, carrying her to my room, and demanding she tell me everything. Instead, I kept my composure and waited for her to check on Kalen before following her to my room.

She sat down on the bed and clasped her hands together while keeping her eyes focused on the floor. "I need to talk to you," she started, and I could tell she was nervous.

"About what?" I asked calmly.

She exhaled heavily and took a moment to choose her words. "I guess I should start from the beginning. A few weeks ago, my half brother showed up at Stuff It and asked if he could use a unit to put his stuff in while he served thirty days in jail. He also asked me if I would take care of his son while he was gone."

"So, Kalen is your nephew?"

"Yes," she confirmed. "I'm sorry for lying to you. I don't know why, but he asked me not to tell anyone Kalen was his son. Anyway, I'd just met you, and I had no idea we'd start dating."

I nodded in understanding. That made sense in a way. He'd asked her not to tell anyone, and I was a complete stranger. "Why are you telling me now?"

"Because the boxes we moved today belong to him. And when I opened the ones that got wet, I think I found something I shouldn't have," she hedged.

"What did you find?" I asked.

She visibly swallowed and clasped her hands even tighter. "Guns," she said so quietly I almost didn't hear her. "A lot of guns." She looked up at me with worry-filled eyes. "I don't know what to do."

"What makes you think you need to do anything?"

"I know those guns aren't his. There were thousands of dollars worth of them. Ben doesn't have that kind of money."

"You think he stole them?" I asked.

"I really don't know, but it's the only thing that makes sense to me. Landon pointed out it wouldn't be hard for someone to make the connection between me and Ben. What if someone comes looking for them?"

"What's your brother in jail for?" I asked.

"He said he missed a court date and had to serve thirty days."

I pulled out my phone and sent a text to Spazz

asking him to come to my room with his laptop. He knocked on the door less than a minute later. "What can I do for you?" he asked as he took a seat.

"I need you to find out why someone's in jail," I said and turned my attention to Blakely. "What's your brother's name?"

"Benjamin Dover."

Spazz's head shot up and he started to laugh, but he stopped abruptly when he realized no one else was laughing. "You're serious?"

"Yes, why?" she asked.

"Because your brother's name is Ben Dover. I thought it was a joke," he explained.

"Oh," she said as realization dawned. "Sorry, I guess I'm used to it."

"Let me see what I can find. He's in Ritch County?"

She shrugged. "I'd assume so, but I really don't know."

"I can't find anything indicating your brother is currently incarcerated," Spazz said after a few minutes of searching.

"What about the court date he missed?" I asked.

Spazz shook his head. "He has a couple of traffic violations but nothing recent. No criminal charges or court dates anywhere in the state of Tennessee."

"If he's not in jail, then where the hell is he?" Blakely almost shouted.

"Can you find a last known address?" I asked Spazz. "Or anything that might help us locate him?"

Spazz nodded. "I can try. It'd be helpful to have

some more information about him—birthday, middle name, stuff like that."

Blakely gave Spazz what she could, but it wasn't much. "Sorry, we aren't very close," she admitted, sounding embarrassed.

"I'll see what I can find and get back to you in a bit," Spazz said before leaving my room.

"What now?" Blakely asked. She seemed completely lost.

"I think we need to go back to Stuff It so I can take a look at those guns. I also think we should move them back to the storage unit, along with anything else that might be problematic," I suggested.

Blakely's forehead wrinkled as she processed my words. "Are you saying we should go through the rest of his stuff?"

"It's the only way to know for sure what you have in your office building. And we might come across something that will help us find him."

"Yeah, I guess you're right," she said and ran her hand over her face. "I can't believe he would do this to me."

"Why not?"

"Well," she sputtered, "because…because…"

"Because you wouldn't do it to him?" I guessed.

"Yeah, I guess so."

"Don't expect people to treat you the way you'd treat them, especially family. It'll only set you up for a lifetime of hurt and disappointment."

"You're speaking from your own experiences, aren't you?"

"Yeah, I am," I said and grabbed her hand to lead her out the door. I didn't want to talk about my fucked-up family right then. In all honesty, I never wanted to talk about them, but I had a feeling we'd be discussing them sooner rather than later. She'd shared a part of her life with me, and it was only fair that I shared some of mine with her.

* * *

I COULD TELL BY THE WAY BLAKELY WAS DRAGGING HER feet that she did not want to go through her brother's things. I wasn't sure if it was because she felt like it was a violation of his privacy or if she was afraid of what else we might find. Regardless, it had to be done, and it seemed like she'd at least come to terms with that on the short drive to Stuff It.

"Which ones have the guns?" I asked once we entered the apartment.

"Those two over there," she said and pointed out the boxes.

I walked over and opened one of the boxes to peer inside. She hadn't been exaggerating. It was full of handguns. I wasn't about to touch any of them, but the ones I could see were clearly missing serial numbers. I took a picture with my phone before moving to the next box, finding it to be full of unmarked guns as well. "Son of a bitch," I muttered to myself and took another picture.

"What?" Blakely asked, causing me to startle. I

hadn't realized she was right beside me, watching my every move.

"Based on the amount he has and the fact that the serial numbers have been removed, I think it's safe to say your brother is somehow involved in gunrunning."

"If that's true, why would he leave them here and disappear?"

"I don't know," I said honestly. "But whatever his reason was, it can't be good."

She shook her head and pinched the bridge of her nose. "I can't believe this is happening. Why would he do something like this to me?"

"Let's worry about the why of it later. Right now, we need to see what else he might have and get it back to the storage unit. Then, we can figure out what to do next."

I'm not sure what changed, but Blakely was no longer apprehensive about going through Ben's boxes. She turned and got to work, going through box after box with no hesitation.

We worked together in a comfortable silence for a while before she spoke. "Let me know if you come across any papers pertaining to Kalen, like his birth certificate or social security card."

"Okay. I haven't seen anything like that yet," I said and paused, unsure if I should ask the question that'd been lingering in the back of my mind since she told me Kalen was her brother's child. But I really wanted to know. "Where is Kalen's mother?"

She looked up from the box she was digging through and met my eyes. "I honestly don't know. Ben told me he didn't even know he had a kid until he found Kalen on his doorstep with a note and a few boxes. He said the note said she didn't want to be a mother and Kalen was his problem to deal with."

"How long ago was that?"

"I didn't specifically ask, but it sounded like it was right before he was supposed to turn himself in for his jail sentence," she said and covered her face with her hand, inhaling deeply. "He dumped his kid on me, didn't he?"

"It kind of seems that way, but why would he leave all of his stuff here if he wasn't planning on coming back?"

"I don't know, but the more I think about it, the more I think he's not planning on coming back," she said.

"That's a lot of money to leave behind," I said and pointed to the guns.

"I think he dumped those on me too."

"What do you mean?" I asked.

"If he stole them and couldn't sell them, the next logical move would be to get rid of them, or in this case, hide them and disappear, right?"

"Maybe," I said slowly. "But I don't think we should waste too much time or energy speculating just yet. Let's see if we find anything here. Then, we'll go back to the clubhouse and talk to Spazz about doing some more in-depth searches, maybe from a different angle."

"A different angle?" she asked curiously.

"Yeah," I nodded. "He should be able to find out

who Kalen's mother is from his birth records. Maybe she knows something that could help us find Ben."

"He can find Kalen's birth records?"

I grinned. "I'm pretty sure he can find anything. And if he can't, we have a friend in Croftridge who can."

15

BLAKELY

We finished searching through Ben's belongings, but we didn't find anything useful. I wasn't sure if I was disappointed or relieved by that. On one hand, I was glad we didn't discover anything else incriminating, but I would have liked to have found some more information regarding Kalen.

"What should we do now?" I asked, hoping Grant would know what to do. Because I sure as hell didn't.

"I think we should take the boxes of guns back to the storage unit and cover them with a tarp," he suggested.

"And then what?"

"Then, we leave them there until we can find your brother or figure out something better to do with them."

It seemed like the best option, so I nodded in agreement.

Grant took care of moving the guns back to the storage unit while I waited in his truck lost in my thoughts. I was wracking my brain trying to think of where Ben could be and how to go about finding him, but I didn't have the first clue because I knew very little about my brother. And what I thought I knew clearly wasn't true.

"You okay?" Grant asked when he returned to the truck.

"Yeah," I sighed. "I was trying to think of where Ben could be and realized I don't know anything about him. Not really." I laughed, but there was no humor in it. "How is that possible? He's my brother."

"Society puts a lot of weight on the word family. But being a blood relative and being family aren't the same thing. Being related to him doesn't mean you have any obligation to him."

I thought about his words as we drove back to the clubhouse. And the more I thought about it, the more I realized he was right. My grandparents were family. Landon was family. Kalen was family. My parents and Ben were not.

Landon and Spazz were waiting for us in the common room when we returned. "How did it go?" Landon asked carefully.

I shook my head. "We didn't find anything else."

"That's a good thing, right?"

"I guess so," I sighed and took a seat beside him. "Where's Kalen?"

He held up the baby monitor and passed it to me. "He's asleep in Game's room. He went down about thirty minutes ago."

"What about you?" Grant asked Spazz. "Have you been able to find anything helpful?"

Spazz shrugged. "I found his last known address, but since he put all of his stuff in storage, I'd assume he isn't living there anymore. I've also got the make and model of his car, as well as his license plate number, which won't be very helpful unless we were utilizing the police to locate him. I do have an address and phone number for a Tracy Peterson—"

I gasped as soon as he said her name and quickly covered my mouth with my hand.

"Does that name mean something to you?" Grant asked and placed his hand on my shoulder.

I inhaled deeply and nodded. "Yes, she's his mother. I mean, our mother." I clasped my hands together tightly and tried to compose myself. I should have expected her name to come up during the search for information on Ben, but I hadn't, and hearing it caught me off guard.

If Spazz noticed how rattled I was, he didn't let it show and continued on with his questions. "Is Richard Dover his father?"

"Yes," I confirmed while Grant shook his head and tried to stifle a laugh. "What?"

"I'm sorry," he chuckled and waved his hand for Spazz to continue. "Tell us what you know about Ben Dover's dad, Dick Dover."

I tried not to laugh. I really did. But Landon's loud guffaw had me cracking up with the rest of the table.

"I've got an address and phone number for him as well," Spazz told us when our laughter died down. He wrote down the information on a piece of paper and handed it to me.

I quickly folded it and shoved it into my pocket. I'd never had any contact with my mother. Not any that I could remember. Obviously, I knew she existed, but I'd never looked for her. I hadn't wanted to. But suddenly, she was a phone call away. I wasn't sure what to do with that information and needed some time to process it.

"Thank you," I finally managed to say. When I looked up, Grant and Landon were both watching me, and I knew I'd have more questions to answer later.

"What about Kalen's birth records?" Grant asked. "Do you think you could find those and tell us who his mother is?"

Spazz nodded. "I should be able to. What's his date of birth?"

"I don't know the exact date. Ben told me he was three months old when he dropped him off," I explained.

"Do you know where he was born?" Spazz asked.

I shook my head. "I don't know anything other than his name," I said and stopped abruptly as something occurred to me. "Ben never said Kalen's last name was Dover. That's an assumption I made."

"That's okay. As long as Ben is listed as the father, I should be able to find his records."

"What if he's not?" I asked.

Spazz grimaced. "That will make things more complicated. The more information I have, the easier it will be to find."

"Thanks, Spazz," I said and pushed back from the table. "I'm going to go check on Kalen."

"I'll come with you," Landon said and got to his feet.

"Are you okay?" he asked as soon as we were behind Grant's closed door.

"Yeah, I'm good," I said quietly, even though I wasn't sure that was entirely true.

"You don't have to talk to her," he said knowingly.

"Yes, I do. She might know where Ben is or be able to help us find him."

"Right, but *you* don't have to talk to her. I can call, or Game can, whichever you prefer. And if someone needs to go knock on her door, we can be the ones to do that too," he said and wrapped his arms around me.

I returned his hug and rested my head against his chest. "Thank you," I whispered. I wanted to say so much more. Thank you for knowing what was wrong and finding a solution so I didn't have to say it and ask for help. But I knew those words would come with tears, and I really didn't want to have a breakdown in the middle of the Blackwings clubhouse with my nephew sleeping a few feet away.

"Do you want me to take that paper from you?"

"Yes! It feels like it's burning a hole in my pocket," I said and handed it to him.

He took it from me and slid it into his own pocket. "Let me know what you want me to ask and when you want me to call."

I looked down at Kalen and back to Landon. "Let's call after he wakes up and has had his bottle."

"Sounds good to me," he said and left the room.

I fell back on the bed and covered my eyes with my

arm. I had so many questions, and none of them had easy answers. Where was Ben? Why did he have all those guns? Why did he lie about going to jail? But the one question that was bothering me the most was: What do I do if he doesn't come back?

I heard the door open and close before I felt the bed depress as Grant laid down beside me. "You okay?"

"Yeah, I was just thinking."

"About?"

I waved my hand in the air. "All of this bullshit with my brother. I can't believe he did this to me."

"It may not seem like it right now, but it's good you figured out what's going on."

"But I haven't figured out what's going on," I countered.

"You may not know all the details, but you know he lied to you. And that's better than not knowing."

"Yeah, I guess you're right," I sighed. "I'm not sure what to do next."

"I think you should try to contact his parents and see if they've heard from him or know where he is," he said.

I pressed my lips into a thin line and scrunched my nose at the thought of speaking with the woman who gave birth to me.

"You don't agree?" he asked.

"It's not that," I started and took a moment to choose my words carefully. "I can't remember any interactions I had with my mother; I was too young. And I'm not sure I want to talk to her. She left me, and I'm okay with that. I really am. But," I paused and took a deep breath, "I don't want speaking to her to change that."

He nodded in understanding. "I don't see why you have to be the one to contact her to ask about Ben. Landon or I can do it," he offered.

"Thanks," I smiled. "Landon pretty much said the same thing."

"Do you think you should let your grandparents know what's going on?" he asked.

"No, not yet. I called them this morning and told them about the damage to the roof, but I think I should wait to tell them about Ben until I have more to tell. I don't want to worry them." Truthfully, I didn't want to disappoint them, and telling them I'd blindly agreed to help Ben would disappoint them. They'd kept me away from that side of my family when I was too young to make the decision for myself and advised me not to get involved with them when I was old enough to make my own choices.

"Why don't I go ahead and call Tracy and Richard? Get it out of the way so you don't have to worry about it anymore," he suggested.

I nodded in agreement. "Thank you."

16

GAME

I left Blakely in my room with Kalen and stepped out to the common room to find Spazz, but I didn't see him in his usual spot.

"He's in his room," Bronze told me before I had a chance to ask.

"Thanks," I said and quickly made my way down the hall to knock on his door.

"Come in," he called out.

I pushed the door open, not surprised to find Landon in his room as well.

"You need something?" Spazz asked without looking up from his laptop.

"Yeah, I wanted to get the contact info for Ben's parents."

His forehead wrinkled in confusion. "I gave it to Blakely, but—"

"I have it," Landon interrupted and pulled the folded paper from his pocket. "She wasn't sure about making the call, and I offered to hang on to the numbers until she was ready," he explained.

"I'm going to make the call for her," I said and held my hand out for the paper.

Landon seemed visibly relieved at my words. "I know she'd call if she had to, but I really don't think it's in her best interest."

Even though I didn't know her as well as he did, I had to agree with him. "Do you mind if I make the calls in here?" I asked and pointed toward the common room. "It's too noisy out there, and Blakely's in my room."

"Sure, go right ahead," Spazz said while Landon beamed.

"Any chance you'll put it on speaker so I can listen in?" Landon asked.

"Sure," I said and dialed the first number.

After several rings, a woman finally answered. "Hello?"

"Hi, is this Tracy Peterson?" I asked.

She was silent for a few seconds. "Who wants to know?"

So, I was speaking with Tracy. If it wasn't her, she would've said no right away. I'm not sure who she thought she was fooling, but it certainly wasn't me.

"My name's Grant, and I'm trying to get in touch with your son, Ben. It's rather urgent. Do you know how I can get in contact with him?"

"What'd you say your name was?"

"Grant," I repeated.

"Well, Grant, I don't know what he's gotten himself

into, but you're the second person who's called here today looking for him," she said, not bothering to answer my question.

"So, do you know how I can reach him?" I asked again.

"No, I don't," she insisted. "He's not here. I haven't seen him or heard from him in weeks. I don't know where he is or when he'll be back. So, you can tell Jordan to stop sending people to me."

"Sorry, but I don't know who Jordan is," I told her.

"What?" she asked. "Then, who the hell are you?"

"Like I said, my name's Grant—"

"I don't care. I can't help you. Don't call me again," she said and ended the call before I had a chance to say anything else.

I looked at Spazz and then Landon. "That wasn't very helpful. Should I try the father next?"

When they both nodded in unison, I dialed the next number.

"Yeah," a man answered on the second ring.

"Hello, is this Richard Dover?" I asked and was met with silence once again.

Finally, he sighed. "What do you want?"

"I'm looking for Ben. I believe he's your son."

"Yeah, he is," he confirmed. "What has he done?"

"Nothing that I'm aware of. I found something that belongs to him, and I'm trying to get it back to him," I said.

"I can only imagine what that might be," he mumbled. "Listen, I don't know where he is or how to get in touch with him."

"What about friends or a girlfriend? Other relatives that I could ask?"

He ignored my question and asked one of his own. "Who am I speaking with?"

I decided to try a different tactic, hoping it would help. "I'm Game with the Blackwings MC."

"Oh, this is great," he said derisively. "Does Hook know about this? No, wait. Don't answer that. I'm not getting in the middle of a gang war. I don't know where Ben is. That's all I have to say." And with that, he hung up.

"Did he say Hook?" Spazz asked with a look of concern on his face.

"Yes, why?"

"Hang on," he said as his fingers flew over his keyboard. "Shit. Shit. Shit."

"What?" Landon and I demanded at the same time.

"I think your girl's got a problem. A big one," he said and turned the screen around to show us what looked like a mug shot. "This is Jordan Hooker, aka Hook. He's the current leader of RFG."

"RFG?" Landon asked.

"Reedy Fork Gang," Spazz and I said in unison.

"Fucking hell," I muttered. "This changes things."

Spazz nodded in agreement while Landon sat in stunned silence.

"Are y'all saying Ben is involved in a gang?" Landon asked.

"We can't say that for sure, but since both of his parents mentioned Jordan without being prompted, I think it's probably safe to assume Ben's affiliated in some way," Spazz explained.

"The guns," Landon whispered.

"What guns?" Spazz asked, his eyes darting between me and Landon.

"Blakely found two boxes full of guns when we moved Ben's stuff earlier. It's why we went back. To move them out of the apartment and back to the storage unit."

"Does Copper know?"

I shook my head. "Not yet."

"You need to tell him. Like right now," Spazz insisted.

I pinched the bridge of my nose and inhaled deeply. "Yeah, I know. I mean, I will. Just, give me a second to figure out what to tell Blakely."

"You can figure that out after you talk to Copper. Come on, I'll go with you so he doesn't have to call me in there to look up stuff five minutes later," he said and turned his attention to Landon. "You're welcome to wait in here while we're gone."

"Thanks, but I think I'll go check on Blakely," he said and got to his feet. "I won't say anything about all this, but if you don't tell her soon, I will."

"I have no intention of keeping this from her," I promised him. "But I'd like to have a plan in place before I tell her. Or at least a better understanding of what we're dealing with."

He nodded once and headed to my room while Spazz and I went to Copper's office and knocked on the door.

"Come in," he said and looked surprised when Spazz and I entered the room. He took one look at our faces and asked, "Something wrong?"

"Yeah, I think so," I said and started explaining everything that had happened and what we'd recently learned.

Copper studied the mugshot of Jordan "Hook" Hooker. "Is he still incarcerated?"

Spazz clicked and typed for a few seconds before answering. "No. It looks like he was released a little over three weeks ago."

"That's when Ben dropped Kalen off with Blakely and disappeared," I pointed out.

"Do you think that's a coincidence?" he asked.

"Not at all."

"Me either," he agreed and rubbed his chin. "Until we can find her brother, I think the best thing to do is leave the guns where they are and continue on like they haven't been discovered. Do you think Blakely will agree to that?"

I nodded. "I do. I'm pretty sure she wants to limit her involvement as much as possible."

"If anyone were to find them and ask, she doesn't know where the guns came from or who they belong to, which isn't entirely untrue," Copper added. "If her brother doesn't resurface when his supposed thirty days are up, we'll figure out what to do with them so they aren't sitting on her property indefinitely. In the meantime, we can have Drew hang out at Stuff It during the day. I assume you'll be staying with Blakely at night."

"Yes, I will," I said and hoped Blakely wouldn't mind me staying at her house for the next week or so.

"Sounds good. We'll reconvene next week. Let me know if anything happens between now and then," Copper said.

"Thanks, Prez," I said and headed back to my room to explain the plan to Blakely.

17

BLAKELY

A week had passed since we discovered the guns my brother was hiding. As a precaution, Drew had been hanging out with me and Landon at Stuff It during the day, and Grant stayed with me each night. Thankfully, nothing out of the ordinary had happened, and I hoped it stayed that way.

"Do you have any plans for today?" Grant asked and took a sip of his coffee.

"Yep. The same plans I have every Sunday. I have to do laundry and go to the grocery store," I told him.

"I'll pick up something for dinner on my way home so you don't have to cook tonight."

"I really don't mind."

"I know. And I don't want that to change," he smiled.

I laughed. "I've enjoyed cooking for years. I'm not going to suddenly get sick of it."

"Still, it's good to take a break every now and then."

"Fine," I relented.

"Text me later and let me know what you want me to pick up," he said and got up to give me a kiss. Then, he made a silly face at Kalen to make him smile before he headed out the door.

"You like him, don't you, bud?"

Kalen answered by smacking his little hands together and kicking his legs in his bouncy seat.

"Yeah, I do too," I said and picked him up to move him to his play yard. "I'm going to get a load of laundry started and then we'll go to the grocery store." I knew he didn't understand a word I was saying, but that didn't stop me from talking to him like he did.

Kalen fell asleep on the way to the grocery store, and I hoped he would stay asleep while I shopped.

Luck was on my side, and I was able to finish shopping in record time. However, Kalen woke up as I was pushing the cart out to the car. I knew I only had a few minutes before he would start crying for a bottle, so I hurried to the car to unload the groceries. I was focused on the task at hand and not paying any attention to my surroundings until I felt something press into my side.

I jolted in surprise and turned my head to see a man standing entirely too close to me. I immediately recognized him as the creepy man who came to Stuff It asking about renting a unit. "Get the baby and come with me. If you try anything stupid, I'll kill you both right here."

"O-okay," I stammered. "I'll do whatever you say. Just, please don't hurt us."

He pressed what I assumed was a gun harder into my side. "Now!" he demanded.

I carefully lifted Kalen's seat from the shopping cart and briefly considered running back to the store. Before I could take a step, the man shoved me toward the car parked behind mine. "Get in," he said sharply.

I climbed into the back seat with Kalen, who started to cry the moment the man closed the door. "It's okay, buddy," I said and put his pacifier in his mouth, which he promptly spit out.

"Shut him up!" the man yelled and sped out of the parking lot.

"I'm trying!" I yelled back. I tried to give him his pacifier a few more times, but he wasn't having it. I rocked his seat as best as I could and rubbed his little head. I even tried Grant's fingernail flicking trick, but nothing worked to soothe him.

By the time the car came to a stop, Kalen was still crying, and I was a frazzled mess. I'd been so focused on calming Kalen that I hadn't paid attention to where we were going or how long we'd been in the car.

"Tell me how to open the gate," he demanded.

It took me a moment to realize where we were. Stuff It. Once I did, I quickly rattled off the code.

He pulled through the gate and parked on the far side of the building. Jerking the door open, he told me to get the baby and get out.

"What do you want?" I asked as he moved us toward the office.

"I want what your brother stole from me," he spat.

My heart started pounding in my chest as panic

raced through me. I had no idea what to do, but I thought playing dumb would be better than admitting I knew about the stolen guns and hadn't done anything about it. "I don't know what you're talking about."

I wasn't prepared for the smack he delivered to my cheek. The impact of it almost knocked me off my feet, but I managed to stay upright after taking a few staggering steps back. I put Kalen down and moved a few feet away from him.

"Don't fucking lie to me!" he screamed and swiped his hands across the front desk, sending everything crashing to the floor. "I know he has my shit here!"

"He has a unit here. It's number three-seventy-three. I'll give you the key and you can get whatever you want out of it."

He hit me again, much harder than the time before. I stumbled back and fell to the ground, instinctively curling into a ball and covering my head. I braced for another hit, but thankfully, it never came.

"I'm not talking about the guns, you stupid bitch. Where's the rest of it?"

I really didn't know what he was talking about, but I wasn't about to tell him that. "The rest of Ben's stuff is upstairs," I said and pointed toward the apartment above us.

He grabbed my arm and yanked me to my feet. "Let's go."

I left Kalen wailing in his car seat while I led him to the apartment upstairs. Once inside, he shoved me to the ground and told me to stay put while he started emptying Ben's boxes.

I had no idea what he was looking for, and I didn't care. I just wanted to get Kalen and get away from him. As he searched through the boxes, I slowly inched my way to the door. If I could get downstairs and get Kalen, I could run to my house or to Landon's and call for help.

I was two feet away from the door when he noticed me. "I thought I told you to stay put." With that, he started kicking me. Over and over. Until he knew I wouldn't try to move again. Because I couldn't.

"Please don't hurt the baby," I whispered and curled into a ball, trying to protect myself as best I could from his relentless onslaught of kicks.

I could barely breathe when he finally stopped and turned back to the boxes. "I know it's here somewhere!"

I didn't know how long I'd have before his attention returned to me, but I couldn't lay there and let him beat me to death. I had to do something.

Cracking my eyes open, I scanned the room for anything that could help me. Hope bloomed in my chest when I saw the weapon my grandfather made a few feet away.

I slowly and painfully dragged myself across the floor until I could wrap my hand around the handle. Then, I pushed myself up using the wall for support. With the last bit of strength I had, I swung the club at his head as hard as I could, hoping to pierce his skull with the protruding screws. My aim was true, and a sickening thud echoed through the room when it made contact with his head.

I screamed in pain while he stumbled backward and fell to the floor. Then, I did the same.

18

LANDON

Lance and I were watching a movie at my apartment when my phone rang with Game's name on the screen.

"Hello?" I answered.

"Hey, man, is Blakely with you?" he asked.

"No, should she be?" I asked in confusion.

"She said she was going to the grocery store earlier, but I haven't been able to get in touch with her all day. She's not answering my calls or texts," he explained.

"That's not like her," I said.

"I know. That's why I called. Can you go over to her house and check on her?"

"Yeah, I'll go right now. I'll call you in a few minutes."

"Thanks, man."

"What's going on?" Lance asked, already on his feet.

"Blakely's not answering her phone, so I'm going to go over and see if she's home."

"I'll go with you," he said and followed me out the

door. Normally, I would have walked to her house, but I didn't want to waste time in case something was wrong, so Lance drove us over in his truck.

Her car wasn't in the driveway, but I knocked on the door anyway. When she didn't answer, I used my key and let myself in.

"Blakely!" I called out. "Are you home?"

I started to go inside, but Lance stepped in front of me with his gun drawn and told me to wait outside. I shook my head. "I'll stay behind you, but I'm going in with you."

Thankfully, he didn't argue with me, and we quickly cleared the house. Even though there was no sign of trouble, I had a bad feeling. "We need to go over and check the office. Something isn't right."

"After you," Lance said.

I took off running across the yard to Stuff It with Lance right behind me. When we reached the gate, I entered my code to open it and cursed the damn thing for being so slow. As soon as it opened wide enough, I slipped through and bolted for the front door. Lance caught up to me and pushed his way in front of me. "Let me go in first," he said quietly and pointed to a car I hadn't noticed parked off to the side of the office.

Lance entered the building and scanned the area. I stepped inside behind him and immediately noticed Kalen in his car seat on the floor. He wasn't actively crying, but it was obvious he had been. His little face was red and covered in snot and tears.

"Take him outside and call Game while I check the

rest of the building," Lance said quietly. "If you hear something, get him out of here."

I didn't want to, but I agreed with a reluctant nod. "Please be careful," I whispered. Then, I did as he said and took Kalen outside. I walked around to the side of the office to shield us from view and took Kalen out of his seat. He nuzzled against my chest and whimpered while I held him close and called Game.

"Did you find her?" he asked as soon as he picked up.

"No," I said quietly. "You need to get over here right now. We found Kalen alone in the office and there's an unfamiliar car parked outside. Lance is still inside looking and I'm outside with Kalen."

"I'm on my way," he said and ended the call. But the relief I'd hoped for at hearing his words didn't come. Instead, I stood there scared as hell, holding Kalen and feeling completely helpless.

Finally, after what felt like an eternity, I heard Lance call my name. I stepped out from my hiding spot and saw him standing at the front door. "She's upstairs," he said and motioned for me to come inside.

"Is she hurt?" I asked and hurried after him.

"Yes," he said matter-of-factly. "I've already called an ambulance. Did you call Game?"

"Yeah, he's on his way. How bad is she hurt?"

"I don't know. She's not completely conscious," he said and hesitated at the door to the apartment. "I don't know what happened, but there's a dead body in there. And it's pretty gruesome. So, try not to look to the right."

"I don't care. Just let me see my B," I said and pushed past him.

Right inside the door, my best friend was crumpled on the ground. Her face was covered in bruises, and her clothes were splattered with blood. "Oh, B," I cried and dropped to the floor beside her. "You're going to be okay. We're here and help is on the way."

"I'll take him," Lance said softly and reached for Kalen.

I scooted as close as I could to Blakely and took her hand in mine while I continued to talk to her with reassuring words. I didn't know how to help her, and I desperately wished she would wake up and tell me that she was going to be okay.

As I stared at my best friend, watching for any signs of consciousness from her and waiting for help to arrive, I had to know who hurt her. Despite Lance's warning, I turned to look at the body on the floor. He was right. The sight was gruesome, but it didn't bother me like I thought it would. If anything, seeing what Blakely did to him provided me with a bit of satisfaction. She'd used the makeshift mace her grandfather made with an old shovel handle and some drywall screws and hit her attacker in the head. He'd fallen to the ground with the weapon still stuck to the side of his face.

"You did good, B," I said proudly, hoping she could hear me.

We heard the sirens and the sound of motorcycles at the same time, and we both sagged with relief. Moments later, the place was filled with bikers, first responders, and police officers.

Blakely came to as they were moving her onto a stretcher. Her eyes popped open and frantically darted around the room as she tried to sit up. "Kalen!" she shouted.

"He's right here," I said and moved to her side so she could see him. "He's okay."

She exhaled in relief as a few tears spilled down her cheeks. "He needs to eat and probably needs his diaper changed," she said and let her head drop back onto the pillow.

"I'll take care of him," I promised. "And then I'll bring him to the hospital. We'll be right behind you."

"You'll need the car seat base. It's in my car."

"Where is your car?" Game asked.

Her forehead wrinkled as she thought. "I guess it's still at the grocery store. Well, I hope it is."

"Don't worry about it right now. Let them take you to the hospital. There are plenty of people here to handle everything else. And I'll be there as soon as I get Kalen situated," I promised.

"Thank you," she said softly and reached out to squeeze my hand.

I leaned down and kissed the top of her head. "Anytime, B. I'll see you soon."

19

BLAKELY

I'm not sure what they gave me in the ambulance, but it knocked me out. When I woke up several hours later, I was in a hospital room with Grant on one side and Landon on the other.

"He's asleep in his seat," Grant said and pointed across the room where Kalen was situated between Spazz and Copper before I had a chance to ask.

"How are you feeling?" Grant and Landon asked at the same time.

"Sore," I said and tried to sit up but stopped immediately when a sharp pain shot through my chest. "Okay, really sore," I admitted. "How much damage did he do?"

Grant grimaced and looked down at his hands. "You have two fractured ribs. Nothing in your face is broken, but you've got some significant bruising and swelling that's going to take a while to go away, as well as a concussion. They didn't find any internal bleeding but want to keep you overnight as a precaution," he said and inhaled deeply. "I'm so fucking sorry, Blakely."

"What? Why? This isn't your fault," I said vehemently and reached for his hand.

"I know. I just—"

"No," I interrupted. "It's not your fault," I said and turned to Landon, "and it isn't yours either. Does it suck? Yes. But it happened and we can't change it. I'm going to be okay, and Kalen's safe. That's all that matters."

Before either one of them could respond, Copper cleared his throat and walked over to my bed. "Now that you're awake, the cops aren't going to wait long to talk to you."

I nodded in understanding. "What do you want me to tell them?"

He grinned. "The truth. Everything except the part about the guns."

"When I mentioned those, he said he didn't care about the guns and was looking for something else."

Copper's eyebrows raised. "Did he say what it was?"

"I don't think so. When I told him I didn't know what he was talking about, he lost his shit and all of this happened," I said and used my hand to gesture to the bruises scattered all over my body.

Copper rubbed his chin thoughtfully. "I'll work on figuring that out. Since Game will be here with you tonight, I'll have Spazz and Drew stay at your house to keep an eye on things."

My eyes widened in surprise. "Why? Do you think

someone else will come looking for whatever he thought I had?"

"I can't say for sure without knowing what he was looking for, but I'd rather err on the side of caution. And, well, Blakely, you killed the leader of a gang. You're going to need protection until we get this sorted," he said bluntly.

"But he attacked me!" I shouted and immediately wished I hadn't when pain erupted in my torso.

"You don't have to defend your actions to anyone here. You did exactly what you needed to do to make sure you and your nephew were safe. We just need a few days to make sure everyone understands that."

"What do you mean?" I asked. I wasn't sure if it was the medicine I'd been given or if he was intentionally being cryptic, but I wasn't following him.

"Let me put it this way. There are two chapters of Blackwings. Both chapters are good friends with The Manglers in Reedy Fork. There's no way that little street gang will want to take on three motorcycle clubs."

"What if they do?" I whispered.

He smiled, but it wasn't friendly. "The choice is theirs, but either way, they won't be a problem for you."

And suddenly, I understood. If the gang refused to back down, the clubs would take them out. "Um, thank you?"

Copper laughed. "You're going to fit in nicely around here, Blakely. I'm going to head out and let you get some rest. I'll see you tomorrow."

I looked at Grant once he was gone. "Why did he say he'd see me tomorrow?"

"They think you should stay at the clubhouse for a few days after you're discharged. And I agree," Landon answered for him.

"You know I can't do that. I have to work," I argued.

He was already shaking his head. "Spazz and Drew are going to help out while you're recovering. They were going to have them there anyway to help watch over the place. Two birds, one stone. It'll be fine."

Before I could argue against their plan, two police detectives knocked on the partially open door, and Grant motioned for them to come in.

"Hi, Ms. Collins. I'm Detective O'Brien and this is my partner Detective Higgins. We need to ask you some questions about what happened at Stuff It today."

So, I started at the beginning and told them everything that happened, starting with Ben asking me to keep Kalen and ending with me in the hospital. Everything except the part about the guns. I wasn't sure why Copper asked me to leave that part out, and I made a mental note to ask Grant after the officers left.

"Do you have any idea what he was looking for?" Detective O'Brien asked.

"Not a clue," I said honestly.

"And what about your brother? Do you know where he is or how to get in touch with him?" Detective Higgins asked.

"No, I haven't heard from him since he dropped Kalen off. He told me he was serving time in jail, so he didn't leave any contact information with me," I explained. "Maybe you guys could help me find him."

Detective O'Brien nodded. "We would like to speak

with him, so we'll see if we can track him down. Here's my card. Please give me a call if you hear from him or think of anything else I need to know."

Once they left, I breathed a sigh of relief. I was tired of talking about the events of the day and my entire body hurt. I just wanted to go to sleep.

"Are you okay?" Grant asked.

"Yeah, I'm fine. I mean, as fine as I can be. I'm just tired, and to be honest, I want to go home."

"Try to get some sleep. You don't need to stay awake on my account."

"What about Kalen? Is he staying here with me tonight?" I asked. I didn't like the thought of him spending the night somewhere else, but I also knew I wouldn't be able to care for him.

"He can if you want him to," Grant said. "Or he can spend the night at the clubhouse with Landon. It's up to you."

"It'd probably be better for him to stay at the clubhouse. Is that okay with you?" I asked Landon.

"Of course it is. I'm here to help and happy to do whatever you think's best."

"Thank you," I said and tried to stop the tears filling my eyes.

"Oh, B, don't cry. We'll be fine. It's only for one night, and you'll be there tomorrow," he reassured me.

"I know," I said and carefully wiped the tears from my swollen cheeks.

"I'll text you when we get there and call you to check in before I go to bed," he promised.

"Thank you," I said and yawned.

Once they were gone, I scooted over so Grant could get in the bed beside me and promptly fell asleep.

20

GAME

Blakely had an uneventful night at the hospital and was cleared to go home around lunchtime the next day.

"Why did Copper ask me not to say anything about the guns?" she asked once we were on our way to the clubhouse.

"To keep you out of trouble. You couldn't be held responsible if you didn't know about them," I explained.

She was quiet for a few minutes before she asked her next question. "What do you think Hook was looking for?"

"I honestly have no idea. If I had to guess, I'd say drugs or money."

"Yeah, that's what I was thinking too. But we went through all of Ben's stuff, and we didn't find anything like that. So, whatever it is, I don't have it."

"I think the only way we're going to find out what he was looking for is to find your brother," I said.

"How can one person be so hard to find?" she asked.

"Hopefully, the police will be able to locate him," I said, though I didn't think they would have much more luck than we did. I didn't want to mention it to her since I didn't have anything concrete to go on, but I had a feeling we couldn't find Ben because he was dead. And if I had to guess, I'd say Hook killed him. Either that, or he had fled to somewhere far away and had no intention of coming back.

When we arrived at the clubhouse, Copper asked me to come to his office after Blakely was settled in my room.

"Do you know someone by the name of Dani Summers?" he asked without preamble.

"Yes, she's my niece, but I haven't seen or spoken to her in years. Why?" I asked. I assumed he wanted to talk to me about the situation with Blakely and was caught off guard by his question.

Copper cleared his throat. "I had Spazz do some more research on Hook after what happened yesterday. I also called Boar to see what he knew about RFG. Your niece, Dani, was Hook's girlfriend."

"You have got to be kidding me," I said in disbelief.

"Afraid not. They were both arrested on drug charges a while back. Hook pled guilty and served a year in prison, but the charges against Dani were dropped," he explained.

"What does this have to do with anything that's going on now?" I asked. It was an interesting coincidence, but I really didn't care about Dani's troubles.

"Rumor has it Dani got pregnant so she'd be able to serve her time in a special facility for pregnant inmates."

"Say what now?"

"But then the charges against her were dropped, and Hook was released early," he continued and slid a piece of paper across his desk to me.

I picked it up and could not believe what I was seeing. It was a printout of Kalen's birth records. With Daniella Summers listed as the birth mother of Kalen Summers.

"He's my niece's son?" I blurted.

"It looks that way."

"This doesn't make any sense. Why would she abandon him with Ben?"

"If you do the math, she got pregnant after Hook was sentenced, so there's no way Kalen is his son," Copper said.

And suddenly, it all made sense. "She used Ben to get pregnant, then had to get rid of the baby before Hook found out what she did."

Copper nodded. "It's all speculation, but that'd be my guess."

"My mother called me a few weeks ago and asked me to help her find Dani. She said no one had seen or heard from her in over a month. Two detectives came by the gym asking about Dani after she filed a missing persons report," I told him. "But that can't be right if Dani is Kalen's mother. Ben said she dropped Kalen off a few days before he passed him off to Blakely. And that happened after Dani supposedly went missing."

"Did your mother know about Ben or the baby?" he asked.

"I really don't know, but I suppose I could ask her."

"I don't see why you need to. Whether she did or didn't won't change anything as far as we're concerned," he said.

"True. So, what now?" I asked.

"Now, you go explain all this to Blakely while I wait to hear back from Boar. He's setting up a meeting with whoever is taking Hook's place. Once that's set, we'll go have a word. There's nothing to do until then," he said.

"Thanks, Prez," I said and headed back to my room.

Blakely took one look at my face and knew something wasn't right. "Is everything okay?"

"Everything's fine," I assured her and took a seat beside her on the bed. "Copper wanted Spazz to do some more research on Hook before we meet with RFG just to make sure there aren't any surprises we don't know about. And it was a good thing he did, because Spazz found quite the surprise."

"What did he find?" she asked anxiously.

I didn't know how to break it to her gently, partially because I was still in shock myself. So, I just blurted it out. "My niece is Kalen's mother."

"What?!" she shouted. "Your niece? The one that's missing?"

"That'd be the one," I nodded. "Apparently, she intentionally got pregnant when she thought she was going to have to serve time in prison so she could be placed in a facility for pregnant inmates."

"Is that even a thing?" she asked.

"Yeah, it is. Some places will even let the mother keep the baby with her for up to a year, sometimes longer," I explained.

"So, how did I end up with Kalen? And where the hell is she now?"

"Since Hook couldn't be Kalen's father, we're assuming she gave Kalen to Ben when Hook was released from prison to keep him from finding out she had a baby with someone else. And for her whereabouts, as far as I know, she's still a missing person."

"This is…I don't even know what word to use to describe what this is," she said.

"Ridiculous. Unbelievable. A hot fucking mess," I suggested.

"Yeah," she agreed. "All of those and then some. What are we going to do, Grant?"

"There's not much we can do, other than try to find them."

"What if we can't? What's going to happen to Kalen?" she asked, and I could tell she was on the verge of tears.

"Nothing's going to happen to Kalen. If we can't find Ben and Dani, we're his family. There's no reason he can't stay with us," I told her.

"I hope you're right," she said quietly.

* * *

After Blakely fell asleep, I asked Layla to listen out for Kalen so I could run an errand. Even though Copper said he didn't see any reason to contact my mother, I couldn't shake the feeling that I should pay her a surprise visit. I didn't think much of it at the time, but Dani had "disappeared" several times before, and my mother never bothered to get the police involved or file a missing persons report. So, what made this time different?

I took my truck so as not to alert anyone to my arrival and parked on the street a few houses down from my mother's place. Her car was parked in the driveway, so I assumed she was home. I watched the house for a few minutes and decided to knock on the door when I didn't see anything out of the ordinary.

"Grant, what are you doing here?" she asked loudly, sounding surprised and possibly nervous.

"I came by to see if you'd heard anything about Dani," I told her and tried to see inside the house over her shoulder. "Aren't you going to invite me in?"

She glanced behind her before opening the door and gesturing for me to come inside. "Well, I didn't think you'd want to, but sure, come on in."

Not much had changed since the last time I'd been inside her home. It wasn't dirty, but it wasn't what I'd call clean either. Every surface was covered in knick-knacks, which were covered in a fine layer of dust. Then, a cat appeared from nowhere and tried to rub against my leg. I immediately stepped back and shooed it away from me.

"I don't know why you have to be like that. He's not going to bother you," she snapped.

"I'm like that because I'm allergic to cats. Which you damn well know," I snapped back. The cats were another point of contention between us. Dani loved cats, and I was allergic to them. So, of course, my mother got Dani two cats. Because she didn't want one to be lonely.

"Then, why did you come? You could've called to ask about Dani," she said and walked to the kitchen to fiddle with a pile of unopened mail.

"Because I wanted to see your face when I asked you if you knew Dani had a baby," I said and waited for her reaction. It was better than I ever could have imagined.

Instead of answering me, she turned on her heel and stormed down the hall where she shoved open a bedroom door and started berating my niece. "You had a baby and didn't tell me?" she screamed.

"I-I…what?" Dani stammered. "What are you talking about?"

I appeared in the doorway as my niece scrambled to come up with a lie to feed my mother. "You know exactly what she's talking about."

"You," she sneered.

"Yeah, me," I said pointedly. "You've got a lot of explaining to do."

"I don't have to explain anything to you."

"Take your pick. You can explain it to me, RFG, or the police. What's it going to be?"

Her eyes widened in surprise for a brief moment before she put her hands on her hips and huffed. "What do you want to know?"

"Everything," I said and held up my hand. "But before you start, you need to come with me."

"I can't! No one can know where I am!" she shouted.

"I think you need to leave," my mother interjected.

"Really? You sure about that?" I asked and stared at her with a pointed look.

"Y-yes, I'm sure," she waffled.

"Okay, I'll go. But when the gang she fucked over figures out she's here and comes to kill you both, don't say I didn't warn you," I told her and turned to leave.

"What the hell is he talking about, Dani?"

"Grant, wait," Dani pleaded. "It's nothing, Grammy."

"It doesn't sound like nothing."

"It's not what he says. He's got it all wrong," she lied, and just like every other time before, my mother believed her.

"See, Grant, you're wrong," my mother said as if her word was final.

"I'm not, but I'm not going to stand here and argue with you. I'm leaving. Are you coming with me or not?"

"Yeah," Dani said. "Give me a minute to change."

She went into her room and came back a few minutes later dressed in oversized clothes with her hair tucked up into a baseball hat.

"Is that your idea of a disguise?" I asked as she followed me out to my truck. Something about the way she looked seemed familiar, but I couldn't put my finger on what it was.

She scoffed. "It's worked for me so far." She stopped beside my truck and hesitated before opening the door. "Where are you taking me?"

"To the clubhouse," I said and waited for her to make her decision. I wasn't going to play her games, and she seemed to understand that, because she nodded once before she opened the door and climbed inside.

"What is it you want to know?" she asked.

"Just wait until we get there. That way you don't have to explain it twice."

"Wow. Aren't you worried I'll use the time to come up with a lie to get myself out of this?"

I huffed out a laugh. "You could try, but there's no way you'll be able to bullshit your way out of trouble this time. My mother is the only one who consistently falls for your crap. I don't care one way or the other about what happens to you, but your best bet is to be completely honest."

"You must care a little bit if you're helping me."

I shook my head. She was unbelievable. "Let's get one thing straight right now. I'm not helping you. Finding you and bringing you to the clubhouse is about me, not you."

Her face scrunched in confusion. "I don't understand."

"I know you don't. But you will."

Thankfully, she remained quiet for the rest of the drive to the clubhouse. She was probably trying to figure out what we knew and how much she should say even though I told her to be honest. She'd never listened to me before, so I didn't expect her to when it really mattered.

Instead of parking in the forecourt and taking her in through the front doors, I drove around to the back and used the rear entrance to escort her inside the clubhouse and down the stairs to the basement.

I gestured to a chair inside one of the rooms. "Have a seat. I'll be back in a few minutes." With that, I closed the door and locked it, laughing to myself when I heard her start to protest.

"You can't lock me in here!" she yelled.

"I can and I did," I laughed.

Then, I went upstairs and knocked on Copper's office door.

"Come in."

"Hey, Prez. So, uh, I stopped by my mother's house a little bit ago, and well, Dani was there. And now she's downstairs in our basement," I blurted.

"You sure don't sugarcoat shit, do you?" he asked and got to his feet.

I shook my head. "Sorry, Prez. I'm still a little shocked that I actually found her, and now she's here."

He nodded in understanding, and I followed him to the basement. He stopped at the bottom of the stairs and turned to me. "I know there's some bad blood between you and your niece, but she is your family. If you have any reservations about what happens with her, I need to know now."

I didn't need to give it any consideration, so I didn't hesitate to answer. "You can't choose the family you're born into, or even the one that raises you, but once you're grown, you can choose your family. The Blackwings are my family. So are Blakely and Kalen. Dani is not. Whatever happens with her is her own fault and won't be a problem for me."

"Okay, then. Let's see what she has to say," Copper said and entered the room.

Dani stopped pacing the room and turned to face us. "I can't believe you lock—" she started, but Copper cut her off.

"Sit down and shut up," he said sharply.

She glared at him for a moment before she reluctantly complied and took a seat in one of the metal chairs in the room.

"How this goes all depends on you," Copper told her. "If you answer my questions, I won't throw you to the wolves. But if you try to bullshit me, I'll fuck your whole world up."

Her eyes widened before she glanced at me, silently pleading for help.

"He ain't gonna help you, so you can wipe that look off your face."

She visibly swallowed and turned her attention back to Copper. "What do you want to know?"

"For starters, where is Ben?"

"I don't know. I haven't seen him in almost a year," she said. Dani was a great liar, but her answer seemed to be truthful.

"So, you haven't seen him since you got pregnant with the baby you left on his doorstep?" Copper asked bluntly.

She sucked in a breath. "No, I haven't."

Copper leaned back in his seat and studied Dani for a few moments before deciding to lay it all out for her. "No one has seen or heard from Ben since he put all of his belongings in storage and dropped the baby off with his sister. That was a few days after you dropped your son off with Ben even though you were supposedly missing at the time. Also, around the same time, Hook was released from prison. Yesterday, Hook showed up at Ben's sister's place looking for something he said Ben stole from him. Any idea what that could be?"

Dani glanced around nervously as the color drained from her face. "Like I said, I haven't had any contact with Ben since last year. But, um, one time I overheard him talking about taking some guns and selling them."

I watched her carefully. I couldn't explain it, but I somehow knew she was telling the truth and lying at the same time.

"Hook knew about the guns. According to Ben's sister, that's not what he was looking for."

Dani crossed her arms over her chest. "Sounds like you should be questioning Ben's sister, not me."

Copper ignored her comment and continued on. "When was the last time you had any contact with Hook?"

Dani shrugged. "I don't know exactly. Sometime after he was arrested but before he went to prison."

"Now, why would a man's long-time girlfriend go into hiding right around the time he's released from prison? That seems odd to me," Copper mused.

Dani narrowed her eyes. "We broke up."

"Then why were you hiding at your grandmother's house?"

"Because I didn't want to see him," she said. She was doing her best to seem confident, but her fidgeting hands under the table said otherwise.

Copper started to ask another question but stopped when someone knocked on the door. I pushed the door open and grinned when Batta stepped into the room with his trusty bat in his hand. "I heard we had a little bird down here who might need some incentive to start singing," he said and gave Dani a wicked smile. "Name's Batta," he told her and held up his bat. "Bet you can guess why."

"I can't believe you're letting them do this to me," she said and started to cry.

"You did this to yourself, Dani." I had no sympathy for her. I'd known years ago that it would only be a matter of time before she got herself into a situation she couldn't get herself out of. Even though we weren't cutting her any slack, she had no idea how lucky she was to be dealing with the Blackwings instead of another club or gang. "And for the record, no one's done anything to you."

"Yet," Batta said ominously.

She gasped and cried harder, though I suspected her tears weren't genuine. I'd seen her cry her way out of numerous situations. Unfortunately for her, her current audience wasn't interested in her performance.

As if reading my mind, Copper told her just that. "You can cut the shit. Your tears aren't doing anything but pissing me off."

Surprisingly, she didn't try to argue and gave up on her charade. If I wasn't so irritated with her, I might have been impressed with how fast she went from a sobbing mess to an angry brat. "What is it you want from me?"

"The truth," Copper said simply.

"He'll get it one way or the other," I told her. "I already told you your best bet is to be honest. That's the only help you'll get from me, and you'd do well to take my advice."

She chewed on her bottom lip and seemed to consider her next move, but Copper's patience was almost gone. He pushed back from the table and stood. "We're meeting with RFG tomorrow, and you'll be going with us. Perhaps you'll have more to say then."

He only made it two steps toward the door when she blurted, "Wait! I'll talk."

Copper pinned her with an icy glare. "You won't get another chance."

"Understood," she said, seemingly resigned to her fate.

We waited a few beats for her to start talking, but she didn't. "The question-and-answer period is over. I'm not going to pull it out of you. You've got two seconds to start talking or we're done here."

"Okay, okay," she said and held her hands up in a placating manner. "Hook thinks Ben stole some of his drugs. That's what he was looking for."

Copper gestured for her to keep going.

She shifted in her seat and started fidgeting with her hands. "But Ben didn't steal his drugs. I did," she said and shifted again. "Hook was released early, and I panicked. I had to get rid of the drugs and the baby before Hook found out. So, I hid the pills in the baby's things and dropped them both off with Ben. Then, I pretended to be missing so he wouldn't be able to associate me with the theft."

"Why would Hook think Ben took the drugs?" Copper asked.

"Because he'd already been accused of stealing from the gang once. I knew if anything else went missing, they'd automatically assume it was Ben," she said.

The room was completely silent while the three of us stared at her in disbelief.

And then I snapped. I lunged at her, but Batta caught me before I could make contact. "Hook almost killed my girlfriend because of you!" I roared over his shoulder.

"What? What are you talking about?" she asked. She looked scared—terrified actually—but it did nothing to ease the rage burning inside me.

"He was looking for what he thought Ben stole, and he almost beat her to death when he couldn't find it!"

"Rein it in, brother," Batta said firmly.

I took a few deep breaths and tried to get myself under control, but it was a struggle. "Calm down and bargain for the baby," Batta said quietly.

I was too upset to understand what he meant. Thankfully, he realized that and explained further. "I guarantee she'll give you the baby to save her own ass."

I knew he was right. So, I swallowed down my anger and focused on getting my great-nephew away from his crazy-ass mother. We'd still have to contend with Ben once we found him, but getting Dani to terminate her rights would be a step in the right direction.

At my nod, Batta released me and stepped back. "Sorry about that, Prez. I'm good."

"It was expected," Copper said and turned his attention back to Dani. "Hook didn't find the drugs yesterday. Where exactly did you hide them?"

"Most are inside a weighted blanket. The rest are hidden inside a few stuffed animals," she admitted.

"Fucking hell," I muttered.

"Pills, right?" Copper asked and Dani nodded. "How many?"

"I don't know exactly. There should be two large bags in the blanket and five stuffed animals have one small bag each. I think four were bears and one was a pig."

Copper knocked his knuckles on the table twice and stood. "We'll be back."

"Wait! Where are you going?" Dani asked.

"To collect your stolen goods. For your sake, I hope you were telling the truth."

"You're just going to leave me here?" she asked incredulously.

"Pretty much," he said and left the room with Batta on his heels. I followed them out and locked the door behind me.

Copper stopped before ascending the stairs. "I'll have Spazz and Drew box up Kalen's stuffed animals and blankets. I want you to go pick up what they find. We'll search through everything once you get back. And for fuck's sake, don't speed."

"I won't," I promised and kept my word all the way to Blakely's and back.

Copper had me meet him in the basement when I returned with the box. I really hoped Spazz and Drew had found everything because I had absolutely no interest in driving through town with a box that potentially contained illegal narcotics ever again.

Surprisingly, Dani was telling the truth. We found two large bags and five small bags of pills exactly where she said they would be.

"How much do you think this is worth?" I asked.

Copper shrugged. "I don't know. Maybe around twenty thousand?"

"Holy shit," I breathed. "No wonder Hook was pissed."

"He's not the only one."

"I'm sorry, Prez. I can take these somewhere else if you don't want them here," I offered.

Copper looked at me like I'd grown two heads. "There's nothing for you to apologize for. Do I like having a pile of pills in my clubhouse? No. But you didn't bring them here. Well, technically, you did, but you know what I mean. Shit like this happens from time to time. It comes with the territory."

"Understood."

"Good. Now help me get these in the safe. I'll feel better once they're locked away."

After Copper closed the door to the safe, he turned to me with an appraising look and laughed. "Go ahead and ask whatever it is before you explode."

I laughed, embarrassed that he'd been able to read me so easily. "I was just wondering what happens next."

"I need to call the brothers in for church. We'll go

over everything and come up with a plan. Since all of this revolves around you and your girl, you'll be in there too. Anything else?"

"Actually, there is one other thing," I said. "Batta said he thought Dani would trade Kalen to save herself. Is that a possibility? I mean, can we do that?"

"You want Kalen?" he asked.

"I'm sure Blakely does. And if for some reason she doesn't, then I'll gladly take him. He deserves better than the parents he was given," I said, meaning every word more than I'd ever meant anything. Kalen was a blessing. He deserved to be loved and to be raised in a happy home.

Copper smiled. "I can't make any promises, but if that's the outcome you want, we'll do what we can to make it happen."

21

GAME

Copper called everyone in for church later that evening. I stood to the side while the officers took their designated seats around the table.

"What are you doing over there acting like a wallflower?" Savior asked and gestured to the empty chair beside him. "Have a seat."

"Thanks, man," I said and joined him at the table.

He seemed to know I was slightly uncomfortable. "It's formal but not. Speak when spoken to, but make sure to catch Copper's attention if you have something to say. He doesn't tolerate outbursts, so keep yourself in check."

Copper took his seat at the head of the table and called the meeting to order. Even though the officers had a good idea of what was going on, Copper started at the beginning and went over everything to make sure everyone was up to date on all the details.

"We have a meeting tomorrow with the top members of RFG at a warehouse that The Manglers own. The purpose of said meeting is to make sure they know Blakely is under our protection, as well as Kalen. Since Kalen is Game's great-nephew, he's granted protection as family. Blakely falls under our protection as his caretaker," he said and directed his attention to me. "Or, if you want to claim her as your Old Lady, we can go that route."

Bronze chuckled. "I'm pretty sure that ship has sailed, and it's just a matter of formality at this point."

"He's right. She's mine," I confirmed.

"All right. That brings us to Dani. While she is Game's niece, he's cut ties with her and doesn't want us to give her any special treatment. Having said that, she does have something he wants. Kalen. We're pretty confident she'll give up her rights to her son for a get-out-of-jail-free card. Does anyone have any objections?"

"What do you mean by 'get out of jail free'?" Judge asked. "Are you suggesting we offer her protection as well?"

Copper shook his head. "No, nothing like that. I thought we could return the drugs she stole at the meeting tomorrow and leave her name completely out of it. As far as she's concerned, we can offer to not hand her over to RFG in exchange for custody of Kalen."

"You think she'll go for that?" Bronze asked.

"I don't see why not. She already did it when she gave the baby to Ben. This would just be a formality for her," Copper said and glanced around the room. "Shall we vote?"

It came as no surprise to me that every officer in the

room voted in favor of letting Dani go in exchange for the rights to Kalen.

"What about the baby's father? Is he going to be a problem?" Bear asked.

"I don't think so. If we can't locate him and convince him to sign his rights over, I don't think it'll be a problem to have his rights terminated. He hasn't contacted Blakely and he hasn't provided any financial support since he dropped his son off with her. That should be grounds for abandonment. If it's not, he's associated with a gang that's involved in gunrunning and selling illegal narcotics. I'll call Tina in the morning and ask her to get started on this. I'm assuming you and Blakely want to adopt him?" Copper asked.

"I haven't mentioned anything to Blakely yet. I didn't want to get her hopes up. But, if for some reason, she doesn't want to adopt him, I will," I said.

"Even if that causes problems between the two of you?" Bronze asked.

"If Blakely has a problem with me adopting Kalen, then she's not the woman for me," I said without hesitation. I didn't want to lose Blakely, and it would hurt like hell, but I didn't think that'd be the case. She already loved Kalen like he was her own.

"After we finish up here, we'll go downstairs and present our offer to Dani. If she's agreeable, talk things over with Blakely and let me know what she says," Copper said.

"Thanks, Prez."

"All right, for tomorrow, I want Judge, Batta, Savior, Coal, and Game with me for the meeting. Bronze, Bear,

Splint, and Tiny will stay at the clubhouse. Spazz and Drew will be helping out at Stuff It," Copper said and glanced around the room. "If no one has anything to add, we'll call it a night."

After he dismissed church, Copper motioned for me to follow him, but instead of going to the basement, he went to the kitchen. "She's been down there for a while. I figured we should probably feed her," he laughed.

"Shit. That hadn't even occurred to me," I admitted.

He shrugged. "The comfort of our 'guests' usually isn't a concern, but this situation is a little different. I figured she might be more agreeable if we show her some hospitality."

"It couldn't hurt, but I don't think we're going to have a problem. She's a selfish person. Always has been. If she has the opportunity to save her own ass, I'd be shocked if she didn't take it," I said.

Copper shoved a sandwich, a bag of chips, an apple, and a bottle of water into a paper bag and handed it to me. "Well, let's go see if you're right."

I opened the door to the room with Dani to find her lying on her back on top of the table staring at the ceiling. She quickly sat up and moved to a chair when we entered.

"Hungry?" I asked and placed the bag of food on the table in front of her.

"Thanks," she said and cautiously peeked into the bag. "How much longer are you going to keep me here?"

"You'll be with us until tomorrow," Copper said.

"We'll move you to a room with a bed and a bathroom after we're finished talking."

She nodded and reached into the bag for the bottle of water. "What are we talking about?"

"We found the pills you stole from Hook, and we're going to return them to RFG tomorrow. Normally, we'd hand you over with the pills and walk away. But, in this case, there's another option that might be better for everyone involved," Copper started.

Dani was listening intently, and I could tell she was interested. "What is it?"

"As I understand it, Hook thinks Ben stole the pills, not you. We're willing to return them and leave your name out of it, if you'll voluntarily terminate your parental rights to Kalen," Copper told her.

"That's it?" she asked.

Part of me wanted to sag in relief, while the other part of me wanted to shake her. How could she care so little about the precious soul she brought into this world?

"That's it," Copper confirmed. "If you agree to this, you'll be signing legal documents. And if you try to go back on your word after the fact, you'll be begging me to kill you before I'm anywhere near finished with you. And since dead parents don't have rights, I'll still get what I want."

Dani didn't seem fazed by Copper's threat. "What happens after I sign the papers?"

"Game will take you back to your grandmother's house," Copper said simply. "You keep our agreement to yourself, and we'll do the same. You run your mouth, and we'll run ours."

Dani nodded once. "Okay, I'll sign." Just like that. She didn't even pretend like she needed time to think it over. I was as relieved as I was disgusted.

"I'll have the papers drawn up tomorrow," Copper said. "It'll be late afternoon, and then you can go home. Oh, and I'll send somebody down to move you to another room soon." We left the room without another word.

"I'm not sure how to feel about what just happened," I admitted once we were back upstairs.

"I know what you mean," Copper said and clapped me on the shoulder. "Go talk with Blakely and let me know what she says."

I walked down the hall to my room and found Layla sitting on the floor playing with Kalen, but Blakely was nowhere in sight. "She's in the shower," Layla said before I could ask.

"By herself?"

"No, Landon's in there in case she needs help," she said.

I turned on my heel intending to barge in there and demand to know what the fuck was going on but stopped myself. Landon was her best friend, and I knew he wasn't interested in her like that. Hell, Landon wasn't interested in girls at all. And Blakely was likely more comfortable with him helping her than someone she hardly knew, like Layla or one of the other Old Ladies.

I calmly knocked on the door before cracking it open. "Everything okay in here?"

"She's almost finished," Landon said and hopped off the counter. "You want to take over?"

"Sure," I answered quickly, causing him to laugh as he left the room.

"You doing okay?" I asked through the shower curtain.

"Not really," she admitted. "I think this was a bad idea. I could only use one hand to wash my hair, and even that was painful. Maybe I'll try a bath next time."

I helped her step out of the shower and dry off. The bruises covering her body had darkened to a deep purple, but the swelling around her eye and cheek appeared to have gone down some. Still, I couldn't believe she was out of bed, let alone up and showering.

"How was your day?" she asked once she was dressed.

"Eventful," I admitted. "I need to talk to you about a few things once you're settled."

"Do you mind if I take Kalen out to the common room for a bit?" Landon asked while I helped Blakely into bed. I don't know how he could have known, but it seemed like he knew we needed some time to have a private conversation.

"Of course not, but he's probably going to be hungry soon," Blakely said.

"Don't worry, B. I'll take the diaper bag and feed him if he starts fussing," Landon promised.

"So, what do you need to talk to me about?" Blakely asked as soon as the door closed behind Landon.

I blew out a slow breath and sat down on the bed beside her. "A lot, actually," I said and shared the events of the day with her.

"You found your niece?" she asked in disbelief.

"Yes," I confirmed. "She's been hiding out at my mother's house."

"I thought your mother reported her missing."

"She did," I nodded. "It was part of their plan to throw people off. I can't say it was a good idea, but it seemed to work. Well, until today."

"Yeah, I guess it did," she said and paused for a few moments. "So, what about Kalen? Does she want him back?"

"That's actually what I wanted to talk to you about. She's going to terminate her parental rights to Kalen. Would you be interested in adopting him?"

Blakely's mouth dropped open in surprise. "What about Ben?"

"Well, it kind of looks like Ben abandoned Kalen. Even if that's not the case, he's involved with a gang. Do you really want to give Kalen back to him?" I asked.

She looked down and started to pick at the blanket covering her. "Of course I don't. But that isn't my decision to make. He's Kalen's father," she said softly.

"And no one knows where he is," I pointed out. "The club has a lawyer. Copper's going to call her in the morning to get the papers Dani needs to sign. If you'd like to work toward adopting Kalen, we can get that ball rolling too."

"What if I say no? What will happen to him?" she asked cautiously.

Somehow, we'd reached the point that could make us or break us. And I wasn't ready. I didn't know how she was going to react, but I didn't have a choice. I had to tell her. "If you say no, then I'm going to fight for him."

She smiled softly and reached out to cup my cheek with her hand. "I love you."

Turning my face, I kissed the palm of her hand before looking back to meet her eyes. "I love you too."

"And yes, I'd like to adopt him, or at least have legal custody of him."

I leaned forward and gently kissed her lips. "I'll let Copper know."

22

GAME

We arrived at the warehouse in Reedy Fork thirty minutes before we were supposed to be there. Boar and a few of his members met us there to let us in.

The place wasn't exactly what I expected. I assumed the building would be empty, but it was apparently being used for some sort of storage judging by the rows of boxes filling half of the space.

"Thanks for letting us make use of your warehouse," Copper said to Boar.

Boar chuckled. "I was more than happy to help. I've been looking for a reason to put these little fuckers in their place for a while now." He gestured over his shoulder with his thumb. "We'll give you some space while you do your thing."

I wasn't sure what to expect, but I had to work to hold back my laughter when five members of RFG walked in. They couldn't have been more cliché if they tried with their baggy clothes and low-quality facial tattoos. Not a one of them could have been older than twenty-five. Any nervousness I'd been feeling vanished at the sight of them.

They stopped a few feet in front of Copper and the one in charge stepped forward. "'Sup? I'm Worm."

Copper lifted his chin. "Copper. President of the Blackwings MC."

"What's this all about?" Worm asked.

"Your boy Hook broke into a storage unit facility the day before yesterday and roughed up the owner. She's an Old Lady," Copper started.

Worm narrowed his eyes. "You saying one of your Old Ladies killed Hook?" he asked with an accusatory tone.

"That's right," Copper confirmed. "She didn't have a choice. He attacked her and she had a baby there to protect."

"She killed our leader. That can't go unpunished," Worm retorted.

"Neither can attacking an Old Lady," Copper shot back and held up his hand. "But we're not interested in a war with you and your boys."

"Then why are we here?" Worm asked and glanced back at his crew.

"From what I understand, Hook was at our girl's place looking for something that Ben stole from him. You know what I'm talking about?"

Worm sniffed and straightened. "I might."

Copper nodded and rubbed his chin. "Hook didn't find what he was looking for, but we did," Copper said and pointed to a box off to the side. "You agree to leave our girl alone, and you can have it back."

Worm looked at his boys and turned back with a smirk. "Sure, we'll agree to that." I knew by the look on his face he didn't mean it. And judging by the rigid posture of my brothers, they did too.

Copper sighed in exasperation. "Fine. Have it your way."

The Manglers stepped out from behind the rows of boxes with guns drawn while we pulled our own pieces. In the blink of an eye, the five members of RFG were surrounded by at least twenty pissed off bikers before any of them could react.

Worm raised his hands in surrender. "Okay, okay," he rushed out. "All is forgiven with your girl."

"Good. My friends and I won't be near as amenable if our paths cross again," Copper said and stepped back. He motioned toward the box. "Get your shit and go."

Worm didn't say a word as he grabbed the box and hurried out the door with his boys right behind him. Still, not one of us holstered our weapon until we heard them peel out of the parking lot.

"You think they'll regroup and try to retaliate?" Copper asked.

Boar laughed and shook his head. "Nah, I think they're about to have bigger problems to deal with. My VP's brother is on the force. He may or may not have received an anonymous tip about a large amount of narcotics being transported through the area."

Copper laughed and held out his hand to Boar. "Remind me never to piss you off."

Boar grinned. "Same goes for you."

Copper snapped his fingers. "I almost forgot. I have

something for you," he said and walked to the back of the truck Coal and I had driven to the warehouse.

Boar signaled for two of his guys to come over and get the boxes of guns.

"Thanks for taking these off our hands," Copper said and extended his hand to Boar.

Boar shook Copper's hand and smiled. "I was happy to help."

* * *

When we returned to the clubhouse, Copper asked me to follow him to his office. He picked up a manila envelope from his desk and handed it to me.

"What's this?" I asked, even though I had an idea of what it might be.

"Tina came by while we were out and completed the necessary paperwork with Dani. Blakely was given temporary custody of Kalen. All of the necessary documentation is in there," Copper said.

"Thanks, Prez," I said sincerely. "I can't wait to tell Blakely the good news."

"You want to take your niece home before you do?" he asked, though I knew it wasn't a question.

"I'd be happy to," I said and headed for the basement.

As I suspected, Dani was more than ready to leave. "It's about time," she huffed.

I rolled my eyes but didn't take her bait. Nothing would come of engaging in a superficial argument with her.

When we reached my truck, she pulled her hair back and tucked it into a baseball hat before she opened the door and got into the passenger's seat. Suddenly, recognition dawned, but I waited until we were on the road to confront her.

"Why did you rummage through the offices at the gym?" I asked bluntly. "It'd be great if we could skip the part where you deny it and pretend you don't know what I'm talking about. I know it was you. You're wearing the exact same disguise right now."

"Does it really matter at this point?" she asked and crossed her arms over her chest.

"No, I suppose it doesn't," I admitted. "But humor me anyway."

She sighed. "I needed some cash, so I was looking for steroids or any other drugs I could sell."

I shook my head. Of all the possible explanations she could have given, that one was probably the least expected. "We don't supply performance-enhancing drugs to our gym members, or any kind of illegal drugs for that matter."

"I'll be sure to remember that," she snapped.

"Would it kill you to show a little gratitude? You've pulled some major shit, and you're basically getting away with a slap on the wrist."

"Oh, please. The only reason it worked out that way is so you could be the hero. I bet you can't wait to tell Grammy what happened," she spat. "How you swooped in to save the day, and now you and your girlfriend will be raising my son."

"Sorry to disappoint you, but I have no desire to

speak to my mother. Now or anytime in the future. I don't need or want her validation. I'm dropping you off at the curb and going on my merry way. Whatever you tell her is your business."

She crossed her arms over her chest. "So, you're not even going to attempt to explain what happened?"

"How many times do I have to say this to you? Your bullshit is not mine. I don't have to explain anything to you or her. And I'm not going to. I don't want to be involved with either one of you, and I've done everything in my power to distance myself from the two of you. Yet somehow, you keep popping up. But this was the last straw. Your selfishness put people I love in danger. I mean it, Dani. I'm done. You and your grandmother need to stay the hell out of my life. You won't like the consequences if you don't."

"Are you threatening me?" she asked haughtily.

Even though I knew she was trying to get a rise out of me, I had to bite back my response. Instead of yelling at her in frustration, I managed to answer calmly. "Yes, very much so, and I have the means to back it up."

"In case you forgot, you're the one who came looking for me," she said.

I honestly didn't know if she really didn't get it or if she was trying to push my buttons. Regardless, I couldn't take much more without losing my composure, and I refused to give her the satisfaction of seeing me come unglued. Thankfully, my time with Dani was over when I pulled up in front of my mother's house moments later.

Or so I thought.

Dani started to reach for the door handle to get out but suddenly jerked her hand back and slid down to the floor in front of the seat.

"What in the hell are you doing?" I demanded.

"What kind of car is in the driveway?" she asked.

"Looks like an old Toyota. Why?" I asked impatiently.

Instead of answering me, she peeked over the dash before dropping back to the floor. "Shit," she breathed. "Shit. Shit. Shit."

I sighed and pinched the bridge of my nose. I had no idea what she was doing, and I didn't want to know. She needed to get the hell out of my truck so I could be done with her once and for all. "Get out and go inside. I need to get back to the clubhouse."

Then, she said the one thing that I couldn't ignore. "I can't. That's Ben's car."

"Are you sure?"

"Yes!" she insisted.

"We've been looking everywhere for that motherfucker. Let's go inside and have a chat," I said and headed for the front door.

"Wait!" Dani hissed from behind me.

But I didn't wait. I was happy that we found him and would finally be able to put an end to the problems he had caused Blakely. I didn't once stop to question why Ben was at my mother's house. Nor did I consider the fact that he might be dangerous.

Instead, I pushed open the unlocked front door and walked into a situation I was not even remotely prepared for.

Ben was pacing the length of the living room and mumbling something to himself when I entered the house. I didn't notice the gun in his hand until he raised his arm and pointed it at me.

"Who the fuck are you?" he demanded.

I raised my hands in front of me. "I'm Grant. My mother lives here."

He used his gun to gesture to the door. "Close it and go sit over th—" He stopped abruptly as his eyes widened and his face contorted with rage. "You fucking bitch!" he screamed and pulled the trigger.

I heard Dani scream as I moved to the side and pulled my gun from the holster at my back. Ben shot at Dani again and turned his aim to me. We fired at the same time. He stumbled backward and fell to the floor as white-hot pain ripped through my arm.

Clutching my arm, I turned to check on Dani and tripped over something on the floor. I lost my balance and fell, hitting my head on the marble coffee table on the way down. My vision swam and my stomach churned with nausea.

My head was throbbing, and it was hard to keep my eyes open, but I was able to get my phone out of my pocket and call Copper.

"Need help," I groaned when he answered. "At my mother's." That was all I could manage to say before I gave in and closed my eyes.

* * *

"GAME," SOMEONE SAID IN THE DISTANCE. "OPEN YOUR eyes, man. Can you hear me?"

I opened my eyes to find Splint hovering over me.

"There you are," he said, and I could hear the relief in his voice.

"What happened?" I asked groggily.

Splint frowned. "You don't remember?"

I tried to think, but I couldn't focus on anything other than the pain in my head. "My head hurts," I mumbled.

"Yeah, I bet it does," he said.

"Tell me what happened."

"From what I can tell, you've been shot, and you have a head injury," he explained. "I was hoping you could fill in the details."

At his words, it all came back in a flash. "Ben," I started and swallowed. My throat was unusually dry, making it hard to speak. "Ben was here. He had a gun. He started shooting, and I think he shot Dani. He got me, and I returned fire. Pretty sure I hit him."

Splint nodded. "Yeah, you did. Do you know what happened to your head?"

"Fuck. This is embarrassing," I grumbled. "I tripped over something and smacked the side of my head on the coffee table."

I grimaced when the stretcher I was on popped up and raised me into the air. "Let's get you to the hospital and see how much damage you did," Splint said and started rolling me toward the door.

"What's the status of the others?" I asked, but Splint

hesitated to answer. "I'm assuming they're dead, but either way, just tell me."

"Ben's dead. Dani was alive when the ambulance left with her, but she was in bad shape. I'm not sure about your mother's injuries," he told me as he loaded me into the back of the ambulance.

"My mother was there?"

"Yeah, we found her on the floor right behind you."

I scoffed. "I bet she's what I tripped over."

Splint nodded. "From what I saw, you're probably right."

I groaned when the ambulance hit a bump and jostled me. "I think I'm going to be sick."

"I can give you something for that, but the nausea is probably because of your head injury, so I doubt the medicine will help."

"Give it to me, man. I can't puke right now. My head already feels like it's going to explode," I said urgently.

"Take some slow, deep breaths," Splint encouraged. "We're almost there." I felt a tingling sensation in my hand and looked down to see him administering something into an IV that I didn't realize I had.

"When did that get there?" I asked.

He chuckled. "Right after we found you knocked out on the floor."

His words reminded me of my desperate call to Copper before I lost consciousness. "Was the club there?"

"Yeah, a few of the brothers arrived about the same

time we did." He pointed out the back window. "And they're right behind us."

I didn't want to lift my head to look, but as soon as he mentioned it, I noticed the sound of multiple motorcycle engines nearby.

"Does Blakely know?" I asked worriedly. I was the one who killed her brother, and I felt like I should be the one to tell her. I just hoped she would be able to forgive me for it.

"I can't say for sure, but I don't think Copper would have said anything to her until he knew what was going on," Splint said and moved to the other side of me. "We're here."

The next few minutes were sheer and total hell as I was transferred from the ambulance to a hospital bed. Every movement made the pain in my skull intensify. And then I did throw up, which only made things worse. "Please make it stop," I begged.

River appeared in my line of sight and reached for my hand. "I've got you," she said soothingly. "You should start feeling some relief momentarily."

"Thank you," I whispered. "You're an angel."

She laughed. "No, I just have the good drugs." Then, she squeezed my hand. "You're going to be okay."

"I am his damn family!" I heard Copper yell from somewhere down the hall.

"Be right back," River said quickly and let go of my hand. "You must be Mr. Summers's uncle. He's been asking for you. Follow me, sir."

Copper appeared at my side moments later. His hair was a mess and he looked frazzled.

"You okay, Prez?"

"Pretty sure I should be asking you that question," he said and exhaled heavily. "You scared the hell out of me, Game."

"Yeah, I think I scared the hell out of me too," I admitted. "Does Blakely know?"

He shook his head. "Not yet. I didn't want to tell her anything until I knew what was going on."

"I killed her brother," I said quietly.

"You didn't have a choice. She'll understand," he assured me. At the look of doubt on my face, he continued, "She herself just had to take a life to defend her own. She will understand."

"Can you have someone bring her up here? I want to be the one to tell her."

"Sorry to interrupt," River said. "We need to take him for a CT scan."

"Blakely will be here when you get back," Copper promised. "I'll tell her the basics and leave the details for you."

"Thanks, Prez," I said and closed my eyes when they wheeled me away.

* * *

As promised, Blakely was in the room waiting for me when I returned. "Oh, Grant," she cried and rushed to my side.

"We're quite the pair, aren't we?" I said, trying to lighten the mood.

"Copper said you walked in on a home invasion at your mother's house. Are you okay?" she asked, completely ignoring my awkward joke.

"I didn't make it out unscathed, but from what they've told me so far, I'll be okay."

"So, what happened?"

"When I took Dani back to my mother's house, Ben was there waiting for her," I said and reached for her hand.

Her eyes widened in surprise. Well, one eye did. The other one was still too swollen to do much. "My brother? He did this to you?"

I swallowed thickly. There was no easy way to say it, so I just told her. "He shot Dani twice when we walked in the door. Then, he shot me at the same time I shot him." I pointed to the side of my face. "This happened when I fell and hit the coffee table."

She gasped and covered her mouth with her hand. "Is she—? Is he—? Are they—?"

It was obvious she couldn't bring herself to say the words, but I knew what she was trying to ask. "Dani was alive when the ambulance got there, but I heard she was pretty bad." I paused and closed my eyes for a brief second before I opened them and met hers. "I'm sorry, Blakely. Ben didn't make it."

"He's dead?" she whispered in disbelief.

"Yes," I confirmed. "He was pronounced dead at the scene."

"Huh," she said quietly. "I'm not sure how I'm supposed to feel right now."

"You're supposed to feel however you actually feel."

"I meant, I'm not sure how I feel. I think I'm kind of pissed at him. Is that normal?" she asked.

"I think you might be in shock. Maybe you should sit down," I suggested.

"Yeah, maybe you're right," she agreed and took a seat in the chair Copper moved to the side of my bed.

Moments later, the doctor came in to tend to the wound on my arm. Between the pain in my head and my worry over how Blakely would take the news, I'd almost forgotten about it. Thankfully, the bullet grazed my arm, so the wound only needed to be cleaned and bandaged. However, I did have a concussion and a skull fracture, but neither required an overnight stay at the hospital.

As soon as the doctor left, the police showed up to get my statement. I told them what I could remember and answered the few questions they had.

Then, River came in and told me I could go home. She went over my discharge instructions, removed my IV, and handed me a stack of papers.

Copper drove us home in my truck that one of the brothers brought to the hospital.

Throughout all of that, Blakely hadn't uttered a word.

23

BLAKELY

I didn't know what to say or do. And I certainly didn't know how to feel. My brother was dead. My brother that I'd never known and never would. My brother who tried to kill the man I loved and probably would have if he had better aim. My brother who left his child with me under false pretenses. My brother who stole guns from a gang and hid them on my property without my knowledge. My brother whose association with said gang resulted in my attack.

The facts were easy to list. I had no trouble acknowledging the things he'd done. What I couldn't do was process any of my emotions resulting from his transgressions.

I wanted to be angry, but what good would that do? Ben was gone and didn't have to face my wrath. Or anyone's for that matter. Anger wouldn't change anything.

I felt like I should be sad, but why? Ben was little more than a stranger to me. His death wouldn't leave a hole in my heart that would be torn open at holidays and family gatherings.

One thing I did feel was relief. I was glad the situation with Ben had finally come to an end. And for that, I felt guilty. My brother was dead. My boyfriend was the one who killed him. How could I possibly feel relieved?

"Blakely," Grant said softly. "Please talk to me."

I blinked to bring my vision back into focus and found him watching me intently. We were back in his room at the clubhouse, and for the first time in hours, it was just the two of us. "I'm not sure what to say," I admitted.

"Say whatever you want. Yell at me. Tell me you hate me. Just say something," he pleaded.

"Hate you?" I asked in confusion. "Why would I hate you?"

"Because I killed your brother," he said quietly.

"You had to. I could never hate you for that," I said truthfully.

"Then what's got you stuck in your head?"

"I feel guilty," I finally admitted.

"What? Why?" he asked incredulously.

"Because I'm not sad. If anything, I'm relieved that this whole mess is over. I didn't want him to die, but I don't exactly feel bad that he did," I confessed.

"Come here," he said and opened his arms for me.

I carefully joined him on the bed, and he wrapped his arms around me. "There's no right or wrong way to feel, but I think you're getting stuck on the familial aspect. Yes, Ben was your half brother, but you didn't know him. You two didn't grow up together and never spent any time together. Essentially, he was a stranger to you."

"Yeah, I guess you're right," I said and smoothed my hand over his chest.

"You've been through a lot the last few days," he added. "It's okay to be okay, but it's also okay to not be okay."

"Is it okay to be sleepy?" I asked and stifled a yawn. Yawning with fractured ribs was a special kind of hell I didn't want to experience again.

"I hope so, because I'm right there with you. Are you ready for bed?"

"No, but I don't think I can make myself get out of this bed to get ready," I admitted. I was exhausted. It wouldn't be the end of the world if I skipped brushing my teeth and slept in the clothes I was wearing.

"Lucky for you, you don't have to."

Before I could ask what he meant, someone knocked on the door.

"Come in," he called out.

Landon walked into the room and smiled. "Well, aren't you two just the cutest little black-eyed peas?"

"Landon," I admonished.

"What? Too soon?" he chuckled.

I shook my head. "You're awful."

"You love me," he said and clapped his hands together once. "Now, where are your clothes? I'm here to get you ready for bed."

"What did you do?" I asked Grant.

"He called for help," Landon answered for him.

"But you need to hurry it up and let me help you because Lance will be here with your bedtime snack momentarily."

I pointed to the bag with my clothes, and Landon made quick work of helping me change into my pajamas. He also plugged our phones in, placed bottles of water on each nightstand, and made sure our pain pills were within reach. Then, Lance walked in with peanut butter and jam sandwiches, crackers, cheese, and grapes.

"Thank you," I said and greedily reached for a sandwich. I didn't even realize I was hungry until food was placed in front of me.

"Clearly, the speech I planned to give you about not taking pain medications on an empty stomach is not needed," Landon teased.

"Definitely not needed. Vomiting doesn't pair well with the broken bones we have," I said between bites.

"That's for damn sure," Grant agreed.

"I'm glad we're joking about all this, but seriously, how are y'all doing?" Landon asked.

"Right now, I'm sore and exhausted," I said.

"It's about the same for me," Grant said.

"How's Kalen?" I asked. "I hope he hasn't been giving you too much trouble."

Landon waved his hand dismissively. "He's been a perfect little angel. He went down for the night without any problems."

"Thank you for taking care of him."

Landon rolled his eyes. "I'm your best friend. You don't have to thank me for doing my job." He reached out and gently squeezed my hand. "Try to get some sleep. I'm right down the hall if you need me."

"You're the best," I said softly.

He grinned. "I know. Aren't you lucky?"

I smiled. "Goodnight, Landon."

"Night, B. Night, G," Landon said and turned off the overhead light before leaving the room with Spazz.

Moments later, we were both sound asleep.

* * *

I WOKE UP WELL BEFORE GRANT. I'D TOSSED AND turned most of the night and finally gave up trying to get any sleep around six. Since there wasn't a lot I could do, I stayed in bed and read a book on my phone in a weak attempt to keep my mind from replaying the events of the day before. I'd been on the same page for at least thirty minutes when I dropped my phone on the bed and blew out a frustrated breath.

Grant reached over and took my hand in his. "You okay?"

I squeezed his hand. "I'm good. How are you feeling?"

"Not great," he admitted. "My head is killing me, but I need to eat before I take anything for it."

"I'll go get something for you," I said and started to get out of bed.

He gently tugged on my hand. "No, you won't. I was given explicit instructions to text Layla when we were up and ready for breakfast."

A few minutes later, Layla and Leigh came to the

room, each carrying a tray of food. "How are you two feeling?" Layla asked and placed a tray in front of Grant while Leigh put one in front of me.

"Sore and spoiled," I said. "I don't think I've ever had breakfast in bed. Thank you."

"You two have earned it," she said. "If either one of you need anything, Leigh and I will be here all day."

"Is Landon here?" I asked. I needed to talk to him about Kalen and work. I knew he would do whatever he could to help, but it wasn't fair to ask him to take care of Kalen and run Stuff It while I recovered.

Layla left the room and returned with Landon and Kalen a few minutes later. My heart melted when Kalen smiled and slapped his hands together when he saw me.

"Hey, little man," I cooed. I desperately wanted to hold him, but I wasn't supposed to lift more than ten pounds. Landon placed him on the bed beside me and it was all I could do not to snatch him up. "How's he been?"

"He's been fine," Landon assured me.

"I'm going to figure out what to do about taking care of him and work."

"It's already taken care of."

"What? How?" I asked.

"I'm going to work open to close for the rest of this week, and Lance is going to help me," he said. "Layla volunteered to help with Kalen, or he can come to work with me. Either way is fine. We'll see how you're feeling at the end of this week and go from there."

I gaped at him, unsure of what to say.

Landon grinned. "Close your mouth and tell me if

you want Kalen to stay here with Layla or go to work with me."

"Are you sure you don't mind?" I asked Layla.

"Not at all," she smiled. "I love babies."

"Glad we got that settled," Landon said. "I'm going to get ready for work. I'll be back this evening."

"Call me if you have any problems," I told him.

"I'll get out of your hair too," Layla said. "Do you want me to take him?"

"He's fine for now," I said. I hadn't been able to spend much time with him since Hook attacked me, and I missed him.

"I'll come back in a little while. Call me if you need me before then."

Once she was gone and it was just the three of us, Grant cleared his throat. "I have some news to share. I was supposed to tell you yesterday, but then all of this happened."

"What is it?" I asked anxiously. I didn't know how much more I could take.

"Dani signed the papers to terminate her parental rights yesterday and temporary custody was given to you. The official paperwork is in Copper's office," he said.

"Really?" I asked in surprise. I wasn't expecting him to deliver good news. "He's mine?"

Grant nodded. "He's yours." He opened his mouth to say something else but hesitated.

"What is it?"

"I don't want it to sound insensitive, but I was going

to say that you can proceed with the adoption process since Ben…" he trailed off.

"Oh, right," I said, understanding his hesitation. Since Ben was dead and Dani terminated her rights, there was no one left to contest the adoption. "Listen, we can't tiptoe around this. Ben's dead, and it's no one's fault but his own."

"You're right," he agreed. "It's still a shitty situation."

It was, and continuing to talk about it wasn't going to do either one of us any good. So, I changed the subject. Sort of. "Did the lawyer say what the next step is?"

"I'm not sure. I'll get her contact info from Copper so we can call her and ask," he said.

* * *

After Kalen went down for a nap, we moved out to the common room for a change of scenery. I wasn't used to not having anything to do, and neither was Grant.

We were trying to decide on something to watch on television when Copper opened the front door and poked his head inside. "Game, you have a visitor. Do you want me to send her in?"

"Sure," Grant said slowly with a look of confusion on his face.

The door pushed open and a girl in her late teens or early twenties who looked vaguely familiar walked in. She took a seat in a chair across from us.

"Can I help you?" Grant asked.

"My name's Zoe, and I'm Dani's sister," she said.

"You mean half sister," Grant corrected.

She shook her head. "No, I mean sister. We have the same mother and father. When they split up, I went with our dad and Dani went with our mom."

"So, why are you here?" Grant asked, seemingly unfazed by the sudden appearance of an unknown relative.

"I wanted to tell you that I don't blame you for what happened to Dani."

"I didn't even know you existed until two minutes ago. Why would you think I'd care if you blamed me?" he asked.

"I didn't know you didn't know about me," she explained. "Anyway, Dani was involved with the wrong kind of people, and what happened wasn't your fault. That's all I came to say."

"I see. Well, thanks for stopping by," Grant said curtly.

My eyes bounced back and forth between the two of them. I felt like I should say something, but I didn't know what. Before I could come up with anything, she stood from her seat and walked out the door.

"She forgot her bag," I said and pointed to the large tote bag sitting on the floor beside her chair. I got up to grab it, hoping I could catch her outside, but as soon as I lifted it from the floor, the bag and everything around it exploded.

* * *

I JOLTED AWAKE AND IMMEDIATELY WRAPPED MY ARMS around my stomach to cradle my ribs as I gasped in a breath. My heart was pounding, and I was covered in a fine sheen of sweat.

"Are you okay?" Grant asked.

I glanced around the room in confusion. It took me several moments to get my bearings.

"Yeah, I think so," I said, still trying to catch my breath. "I had a dream, and it seemed so real."

"Tell me about it," he said and scooted closer to me.

I wiped the sweat from my face and took a few sips of water before I started telling him about the dream.

"I can assure you, I only have one niece. And what happened with her wasn't my fault or yours," he said.

"I know. I'm not sure why it rattled me so much," I admitted.

"After everything that's happened over the last few days, you're probably subconsciously waiting for something else to happen and it's manifesting in your dreams. But nothing else is going to happen. We're safe, and we have Kalen. It's over."

24

GAME

After a week at the clubhouse, Blakely was more than ready to go home.

"It has nothing to do with the club. Everyone here has been great," she assured me. "But I miss sleeping in my own bed, and I really do need to get back to work."

It wasn't quite the same for me. I was used to bouncing back and forth between my place and the clubhouse, and I didn't have the same attachment to my rental house that she did to her grandparents' house. But I understood where she was coming from.

The doctor told her she could increase her activity as tolerated. Other than moving a little slower than usual and being very careful when lifting Kalen, she was up and about almost as if nothing had happened. I knew she'd be okay at home, but I didn't want her to go. Unless I went with her.

"Do you think one of the guys could drive us over to my house?" she asked. Even though we were both recovering well, neither one of us had been cleared to drive yet.

"Us?" I asked.

She stopped gathering her belongings and turned to face me. "I guess that was kind of presumptuous. I just assumed you'd come with me. But you're probably sick of me by now."

"I don't think I'll ever be sick of you," I said honestly.

She smiled shyly. "So, does that mean you're going to stay at my house for a bit? At least until you're healed?"

"Or until you're sick of me," I teased.

"That won't happen," she promised.

A few hours later, Landon and Spazz picked us up at the clubhouse and drove us to Blakely's house. I felt like a chump standing there watching as they loaded our bags and all of Kalen's things into the back of Spazz's truck. But they wouldn't have let me help even if I tried.

Once we were loaded up and on the way, Landon turned in his seat to talk to Blakely. "I have something to tell you, but I want you to remember two things—this was beyond my control, and I'm just the messenger."

"Understood. What is it?" Blakely asked anxiously.

"Nana and Papa are on their way home. They'll get here sometime tonight."

"What?" she asked in surprise.

Landon nodded. "Nana called me this morning. She said she thought something was going on because she hadn't talked to you as much as usual and felt like you were being vague when she did. Then, she checked the cameras and saw that you haven't been at Stuff It for the last week."

"Did you tell her why?"

"I started to, but she stopped me. She said she'd wait to hear it from you, but she wanted me to tell you to be ready to explain yourself," he said.

Blakely groaned. "This is going to be a long night."

"Yep," Landon agreed. "For both of us. She told me in no uncertain terms that I had to be there too."

"So, Spazz, sounds like we're hanging out tonight," I joked.

"Oh, no. If we have to face Nana's wrath, so do you two," Landon said.

"What? Why me?" Spazz asked. "Of all the people in this truck, I'm the least to blame for upsetting Nana."

"That's exactly why you need to be there. She'll love you and Game. Then, we'll give her the baby and hope for the best," Landon said.

The rest of the day was a whirlwind of activity as Blakely and Landon got ready for Nana and Papa's impending arrival. I was worried she was doing too much, but she assured me she wasn't.

"When are they supposed to be here?" Blakely asked.

"She didn't say. She called me around ten and said they were on their way. We can probably figure it out if you know where they were coming from," Landon said.

"They were in Destin, Florida. How far away is that?"

"Around seven hours, but that's without stopping or traffic," Spazz said.

"They'll definitely stop a few times. So, the earliest they could get here would be six or seven," Blakely guessed.

As it turned out, her grandparents pulled into her driveway a little after eight. It was close to Kalen's bedtime, but thankfully, he was still awake and seemed to be in a good mood.

Blakely's grandmother walked in and went right to her with her arms wide open but stopped short when she saw Blakely's face. "I knew something was wrong. What happened?" she asked and proceeded forward to hug her granddaughter.

"She has broken ribs," I blurted.

Mrs. Collins wrapped her arms around Blakely's shoulders and gently embraced her. "Are you okay, sweetheart?"

"For the most part. My ribs will take a while to heal, but they're much better than they were."

"Good. Now, introduce me to your friends. You can tell me everything while I make us all something to eat. I hope y'all are hungry."

"I am," Landon said.

"You always are," she said and laughed. "Come here, my other errant child, and give me a hug."

Landon smiled sheepishly and did as she asked. When he stepped to the side, Blakely started with the introductions.

"Nana, this is my boyfriend, Grant. And this is Landon's boyfriend, Lance," she said.

"It's nice to meet you both. Please, call me Nana," she said and set about giving both of us a welcoming hug.

Blakely turned to give Landon a pointed look. He disappeared into the living room and returned moments later carrying Kalen. "And this is Kalen."

Nana's mouth dropped open in shock. "Where in the world did he come from?"

"It's a long story, Nana," Blakely said.

"Well, you better get to telling it. I'm about out of patience," she said sternly.

"What's that?" Landon asked and lowered his ear to Kalen. "You want Nana to hold you?" He sidled up to Nana and passed her the baby.

She softened immediately. "He sure is cute." She cooed at Kalen and ran her hand over his head. Then, she gave Blakely and Landon a knowing look. "Nice try, but the cute baby won't save you."

"I don't know what you're talking about," Landon said, feigning innocence.

"Where's Papa?" Blakely asked.

"He was getting the RV hooked up, but he should have been in here by now," Nana said.

As if on cue, the man presumed to be Papa opened the door and stepped inside. He glanced around and took in the room. "All right, just what in the hell is going on around here?"

"Sit down, Conway. Blakely is going to tell us," Nana said.

"I know Landon, but who are these other two? And why are you holding a baby?" he asked.

Nana let out an exasperated sigh and introduced me and Spazz to her husband, who instructed us to call him Conway.

"Here, you take the baby while I get dinner started," Nana said to her husband. "Blakely and the boys are going to fill us in."

Blakely was almost finished telling Nana everything when Kalen started to cry.

"I'll get him, so you can keep going," Landon offered.

When he returned, Blakely had finished and dinner was ready. The conversation paused while we loaded our plates and resumed once everyone was seated at the table.

"I'm honestly at a loss for words," Nana said.

Conway smiled. "I'm not. I told you that mace would come in handy one day. I'm damn proud of you for using it, sweetheart. I'll get started on making you another one tomorrow."

"Thanks, Papa," Blakely said with a soft smile.

Nana turned her attention to me. "What happened to your mother and niece? I don't think Blakely said."

"My mother was knocked unconscious from a blow to the head and broke her hip when she fell. My niece was shot twice. She has a long road ahead of her, but both are expected to make a full recovery," I shared.

"I didn't know you'd gotten an update. Why didn't you tell me?" Blakely asked.

"I haven't had a chance to. Someone from the hospital called while you and Landon were getting things ready around here. She wanted to talk to me about taking care of my mother at home once she's discharged."

"Are you serious? What did you say?"

"I told her she needed to come up with a different plan because she wasn't coming home with me. River told me they'd call and try to pressure me into taking her home, so I was ready when she tried to argue with me," I explained.

Nana reached over and patted my shoulder. "It's not easy to cut ties with family, but you have to do what's best for you." I knew she understood. Blakely told me her dad dropped her off with her grandparents after she was born and never came back, but I had a feeling there was more to the story.

"You're right about that," I agreed.

"Is Ben's stuff still in the apartment?" Conway asked.

"Yes, it is," Blakely answered. "I have no idea what to do with it."

"Does it belong to Kalen now?" Landon asked. "Since he's Ben's son."

"I don't know," Blakely said. "I guess I need to find out how that works."

"Sorry, sweetheart. I didn't mean to open a can of worms," Conway said. "I was just wondering if you needed help moving the boxes or sorting through them."

"Thanks, Papa, but I'll get Landon to help me if I need it."

"That's my girl," he laughed.

"Hey, now, I'm not the only muscle around here anymore," Landon said and pointed at me and Spazz.

Nana smiled broadly. "Welcome to the family, boys."

EPILOGUE

BLAKELY

One Year Later

The forecourt was packed full of cars and bikes when we arrived, as it usually was whenever the Blackwings were having a party. I smiled to myself while Grant parked the truck. This party was for us. Well, technically, it was for me. Earlier that day, Kalen's adoption had been finalized. He was officially my son. And since I was Grant's Old Lady, in the eyes of the club, Kalen was his son as well.

The room erupted in cheers when we entered. Kalen squealed in delight and kicked his legs to let me know he wanted me to put him down. I happily obliged and watched him toddle over to play with Sienna and Blue.

"I'm going to grab a beer. Do you want something to drink?" Grant asked.

"Just a water for now," I said.

"Be right back," he said and kissed my cheek.

I breathed a sigh of relief when he didn't question me about the water. He knew how much I loved BWOLs, but I wasn't going to be able to enjoy them for another eight months or so.

I hadn't told him yet, or anyone for that matter. I took the test the day before, but I wanted to wait to tell him until after the final court hearing.

"We saved you a seat," Aspen said and looped her arm through mine.

"You always do," I said with a laugh. Aspen had become a good friend over the last year. We spent a lot of time with her and Coal, as well as Landon and Spazz.

Landon was still my best friend. I was worried things would be different when Grant moved in with me and he moved in with Spazz, but nothing changed.

"Excuse me, is this seat taken?" a familiar and unexpected voice said from behind me.

"Nana!" I shouted and jumped out of my chair to engulf her in a hug. "What are you doing here?"

"Did you really think we'd miss your big day?" she asked incredulously. "We would have been here for the hearing, but there was a wreck on the interstate that held us back a few hours."

"My turn," Papa said and gently nudged Nana to the side. "Congratulations, sweetheart," he said and wrapped his arms around me. "I'm so proud of you."

I blamed the pregnancy hormones when tears started to well in my eyes. "Thank you," I said softly.

"Where's my great-grandson?" he asked, oblivious to my emotions.

I pointed to the corner of the common room we'd started referring to as the play area. "Right over there."

I chuckled to myself when they both ditched me and made a beeline for Kalen. He flashed them a wide, gummy grin when he saw them approaching and stood to waddle toward them. He'd been walking for a few months but still wasn't steady on his feet. Papa scooped Kalen into his arms and turned back to face the room expectantly.

The room fell silent, and I wrinkled my forehead in confusion. When I turned around to ask Aspen what was going on, I found Grant standing there with a goofy smile on his face.

"What are you doing?" I asked softly.

"You know," he replied. I didn't, until he reached into his pocket and lowered himself to one knee.

I stuck my left hand out and was already nodding my head before he had a chance to ask.

He chuckled and opened the box. "Will you marry me?"

"Yes!" I shouted. And before I could stop myself, I blurted, "I'm pregnant!"

He was on his feet and hoisting me into the air in seconds. "I love you!"

"I love you too."

"You need to call someone to come out and test the water," Batta said to Copper.

"What? Why?" Copper asked.

"Seriously? Tatum and Mackenzie had babies last

year. River's going to pop any day now, and Layla's not far behind her. Sloane and Aspen announced pregnancies last month and now Blakely. Something's going on around here," Batta said.

Savior and Avery were whispering intensely to each other at their table but stopped when the attention of the room fell on them. Savior cleared his throat. "We were going to wait to say anything because we didn't want to steal your thunder, but yeah, Avery's pregnant too."

I glanced at Landon who looked like he was about to combust. Spazz gently nudged him with his elbow. "Go ahead," he said.

Landon jumped to his feet. "The adoption agency called this morning. One of their mothers picked us to adopt her baby!"

Copper smiled. "Buckle up, brothers. It sounds like we're in for one hell of a ride."

ABOUT THE AUTHOR

Website/Newsletter Sign-up

Facebook Reader Group

Signed Books/Merchandise

ALSO BY TEAGAN BROOKS

Blackwings MC

Dash

Duke

Phoenix

Carbon

Shaker

Badger

Blackwings MC Box Set

Blackwings MC - Devil Springs

Copper

Judge

Savior

Batta

Bronze

Bear

Coal

Game

King Mountain Shifters

Slade

Standalones

Beached

Christmas in Tinsel Town

Printed in Great Britain
by Amazon

46381136R00136